A Poisonous Play

THE REBECCA ORANGE CASTLE COZY MYSTERY SERIES
SERIES
BOOK SEVEN

VALERIE BRANDY

EMERALD LION
PRESS

🌸 Formatted with Vellum

CHAPTER

One

BEING A DUCHESS, *it turns out, is significantly more nerve-wracking than wrangling wildlife.* I think the words while sitting in the front row of Monrovia's Grand Playhouse, wearing an *actual* tiara. Behind me, two hundred pairs of eyes burn holes into the back of my neck. The velvet seat beneath me feels too hard, and I resist the urge to check if my formal gown is riding up in the back.

"You asked me to tell you if you're fidgeting," Jack whispers, his breath warm against my ear as he reaches over to place his hand on mine, stilling my fingers that have been unconsciously pleating the program into accordion folds. "Does this qualify?"

"I'm not fidgeting. I'm... reinterpreting the structural integrity of paper," I whisper back, but I let the mangled program rest in my lap. "Everyone is staring."

"Of course they're staring. Look at you." Jack's eyes crinkle at the corners as he smiles at me, that private smile that still makes my stomach flip even after months of marriage. "You're the most beautiful woman in the world."

"I'm the most *terrified* woman in the world," I correct him, though I can't help the warmth that spreads through me at his words.

Beside me, Joe shifts his massive frame, the bow tie around his thick neck looking comically small against his golden fur. He lets out a small huff, clearly unimpressed with having to sit still for so long. On Jack's other side, Luma, his elegant collie, sits primly in her sparkly collar, the picture of canine dignity.

"Joe, please behave," I murmur, leaning down to straighten his bow tie. "This is our first official royal outing as a family."

"He looks very distinguished," Maggie— my best friend— says from my other side, her blonde braids elaborately woven with tiny pearls for the occasion. "Like he's about to deliver a TED Talk on the superiority of bacon treats."

I snort, earning a disapproving glance from an elderly woman two rows back. *Great.* Five minutes into my first official event as a royal patron and I'm already committing some faux pas. I can see tomorrow's headlines now: *"New Duchess Snorts Like Barnyard Animal at Shakespeare Opening."*

The Grand Playhouse of Monrovia is every bit as impressive as its name suggests. The building had been lovingly restored over the past year, with its ornate gold-leaf ceiling medallions and plush red velvet seats making it feel like we've stepped back in time to a more elegant era. Crystal chandeliers hang overhead, their light catching and refracting in the jewels adorning the necks and wrists of Monrovia's elite. The air smells of polished wood, expensive perfume, and the faint, exciting whiff of fresh paint from the newly renovated stage.

My gaze travels up to the royal box— where we *should* be sitting, according to tradition— but I wanted to take front row seats instead. I'd feel too stared at in the box, like a bird in a cage on display. Jack heartily agreed with the idea, stating that sitting in the audience, with "the people," was a more egalitarian choice. "If we're going to support the arts," he'd said, "let's actually see the arts up close." This is one of many qualities that made me fall in love with Jack— his determination to modernize without destroying tradition, to be part of the community rather than floating above it.

I smooth down the front of my emerald green gown, trying to look like I belong here. The tiara— a small, tasteful one from the royal collection— feels like it weighs a thousand pounds, though it can't be more than a few ounces. I'd practiced walking with it for hours, terrified I'd send it tumbling to the ground in front of everyone.

"Relax," Jack whispers again, his fingers giving mine a gentle squeeze. "You're doing brilliantly."

"I haven't done anything yet except sit here looking petrified."

"That's basically the entire job. You're– how would you Americans say? You're... *nailing* it," he teases, his eyes twinkling.

I resist the urge to elbow him in the ribs, aware that such behavior is probably frowned upon in duchesses. Instead, I take a deep breath and try to center myself. This playhouse means something to me. It's not just a building; it's a statement about the importance of arts and culture, of stories that connect us across centuries. When Jack had asked what cause I wanted to champion as a duchess, I hadn't hesitated.

"I still think we should have gone on our honeymoon first," Jack says, voice pitched low enough that only I can hear him. "Paris in the spring, Rome in the summer— we could have done the whole grand tour before diving into official duties."

"And leave Monrovia without quality Shakespeare for another six months?" I reply, arching an eyebrow. "I couldn't stand the thought of it. Besides, the dogs would have missed us."

As if on cue, Joe lets out a dramatic sigh and slumps

against his chair. Even in formal attire, he's still my oversized, lovable goofball.

"He's not wrong about the honeymoon, though," Maggie chimes in, leaning forward to look past me at Jack. "Most royal brides would milk that for all it's worth. Three weeks minimum in some exotic locale, Instagram photos on yachts, drinking mimosas for breakfast..."

"Thank you for that helpful input, Maggie," I say dryly.

She grins. "Just saying… if you're looking for someone to take the honeymoon while you two are busy, I'll go by myself. Just out of service to the crown."

"How selfless of you, Maggie," Jack nods.

"She wouldn't have to go alone," I tease, smirking. "I'm sure *Benjamin* would be happy to join her."

Maggie blushes, and suddenly seems very interested in the chandelier floating above our heads. Maggie is shy about her ongoing flirtation with Benjamin, who runs the village pet shop. She's about to open her mouth and change the subject when the chandelier begins to flash: it's a final warning for everyone to take their seats. The show is about to begin.

"Rebecca, it's almost time!" Maggie says, grabbing my arm.

"If I don't end up in the papers tonight, I'll consider my efforts a win," I say, swallowing hard.

"Please," Maggie shakes her head. "You *always* end up in the papers one way or another."

Before I can defend myself, the house lights begin to dim. The murmur of conversation around us fades as the audience settles in. Joe shifts against my leg, and I reach down to place a calming hand on his massive head. For all his size and occasional clumsiness, he understands the concept of quiet time remarkably well.

"I still can't believe they chose '*The Taming of the Shrew*' for their opening production," Jack whispers to me as the lights continue to lower. "It's not exactly the most progressive of Shakespeare's works."

"The director mentioned something about a modern reinterpretation," I whisper back. "I hope they pull it off. Otherwise, the papers will say it's my fault. In fact, anything that goes wrong tonight will be my fault."

The final lights dim, plunging the theater into a moment of perfect darkness before a single spotlight illuminates the heavy red curtains. My heart beats faster with anticipation. Whatever my misgivings about the play choice, there's something magical about this moment— the hush of expectation, the collective held breath of an audience about to be transported.

The curtains part with a soft whoosh, revealing a tavern scene that serves as the play's opening. The set design is impressive— weathered wooden tables, flickering lantern light, and a sense of lived-in authenticity that immediately establishes the world of the play. A man in tattered clothing sprawls across one of the benches, clearly meant to be Christopher Sly, the drunken tinker from the play's induction.

"I'll pheeze you, in faith," the actor slurs, staggering to his feet as the tavern hostess approaches.

The actress playing the hostess is magnificent— her exasperation palpable as she confronts Sly about his drunken behavior and unpaid tab. Their exchange is sharp and funny, drawing appreciative chuckles from the audience. I find myself leaning forward slightly, drawn into the performance despite my earlier reservations.

It's going so well, I think, struck by a moment of pride. *Why was I worried? My first royal patronage is going to be perfect.*

The actor playing Sly lurches around the stage with impressive physical comedy, his movements just controlled enough to show the skill behind the apparent chaos. When he reaches for his tankard on the table, his timing is perfect— a dramatic pause, a wobbling reach, and then a firm grasp that draws another laugh from the audience.

"A sixpence a piece, and I'll pay you!" he announces grandly, lifting the tankard for a deep, theatrical swig. The actor swallows.

Then, he pauses. For a second, I think he's forgotten his lines.

Something changes in his expression. The tankard slips from his fingers, clattering to the stage floor. His body follows a moment later, crumpling in a way that doesn't look rehearsed.

The audience laughs— they think the fall is part of the comedy, a drunken collapse played for laughs. But I've seen enough animals in distress to recognize when something is terribly wrong. The man's face has gone slack in a way that has nothing to do with acting. His limbs aren't positioned to protect himself from the fall— they're completely limp.

Something's wrong with him, I think, but the words are stuck in my throat.

The actress playing the hostess continues her lines for a moment before she seems to realize something's amiss. She approaches the fallen actor.

"Christopher?" she says his character's name. When he doesn't respond, she kneels beside him, her hand on his shoulder, more frantic now. "Tom?" This time using what must be the actor's real name. "*Tom,* are you alright?"

The audience begins to murmur, the atmosphere in the theater shifting from amusement to uncertainty. Joe senses it too, his massive head lifting from my foot as he sits up straighter. Beside him, Luma growls, raising the fur on her back.

The actress's face changes as she rolls the actor onto his back, revealing his unnaturally pale face. "Someone get help!" she calls out, her voice piercing through the confused murmurs of the audience. "He's not breathing!"

Beside me, Jack leans close. "Was that part of the show?" he asks, his voice tight with concern.

I'm already half-rising from my seat, my eyes fixed on the fallen actor. There's a familiar stillness to him that sends a chill down my spine.

"Not from the rehearsals I saw," I reply, my voice barely above a whisper. "Jack... I think… I think... he's been *poisoned*."

The word seems to hang in the air between us as chaos erupts on stage. The curtain begins to lower hastily, but not before we see several stagehands rushing toward the fallen actor. A woman in the third row screams, and suddenly the orderly theater dissolves into panicked confusion.

Joe presses against my leg, his training kicking in as he senses my tension. Luma whines softly from Jack's side. In her typical fashion, Maggie is already on her phone, presumably calling for medical assistance. Maggie is the type of person you want beside you in a crisis, and seeing her snap into what I recognize as her "emergency mode" makes it clear: we're in trouble.

I meet Jack's eyes, seeing my own shock reflected there. Our perfect opening night— my first official function as duchess and patron— has just become something else entirely.

So much for not ending up in the papers, I think.

And somehow, I know with a sinking certainty that this is only the beginning.

CHAPTER
Two

THE STAGE LIGHTS catch the foam around Tom Prink's mouth. It glistens in a way that makes my stomach turn. Beside me, Maggie puts a hand on my arm. "He looks so…" She pauses, thinking of the right thing to say.

"Dead," I confirm.

We're all up on stage together like actors in the world's worst play: Jack, Maggie, and me, with Joe and Luma sitting elegantly at my heel. The dogs are holding it together for once, sitting poised like Police dogs. *Thanks for not running around and embarrassing me,* I silently praise them.

Nearby, Officer Basilier looks at the dogs with a skeptical eye. She's let them up on stage to join us, but the invitation will only last so long as they don't disturb the crime scene. The Monrovian Police have roped off the entire theater with yellow tape and evacuated the audience.

"Well, Your *Grace,*" Officer Basilier smirks at me, using the title with her usual sarcasm. "What a *lovely* first patronage you've chosen. Excellent job exposing the community to the arts! The children in attendance will never forget their first murder."

"I didn't expect anyone to die—" I counter.

Officer Basilier shakes her head. "It's *you*, Rebecca. You should've picked something less public for your first patronage as a duchess. Something safer. Environmentalism, a walk around the trees or—"

I open my mouth to respond— probably with something about how trouble seems to follow me no matter what I do— when a throat clears behind us. The sound is so deliberately aristocratic, so purposefully disapproving, that my shoulders tense before I even turn around.

"I have to agree," the voice says.

It belongs to Mrs. Trechón, my new nemesis. She's standing at the edge of the stage, her immaculate brown hair frozen in place. She's wearing what I've come to think of as her uniform: a perfectly pressed suit, pearls that gleam with the kind of luster that says 'old money,' and an expression that suggests she's just bitten into a lemon.

Not her, I think, biting my lip to keep from saying something I'll regret later. *I thought we left you at the castle.*

"Your Grace," she says, somehow making my title sound like an accusation. "*Qu'est-ce que vous faites*? What exactly are you doing?"

A quick update on my life: This woman has been following me around since Jack and I got married. For three weeks now, Mrs. Trechón has been a thorn in my side. She was sent by the Queen herself to "support" me in my first year as a Duchess. Support, apparently, means criticizing everything from how I hold a teacup to my insistence on wearing comfortable shoes when no one's looking. I can't get rid of her — believe me, I've tried everything short of having Joe accidentally knock her into the castle moat. The Queen's orders are the Queen's orders— and her *orders* are for this crazy woman to follow me around, harassing me into Duchessdom. Mrs. Trechón reminds me of this fact approximately seventeen times a day.

"I'm investigating a murder," I say, trying to keep my voice level. "Someone died at my patronage event and I intend to find out who did it."

Mrs. Trechón's nostrils flare slightly, the only sign that she's fighting to maintain her composure. "Duchesses do *not* investigate murders. Duchesses do not stand around dead bodies. Duchesses most certainly do not—" she pauses, looking at my practical boots with visible disgust, "—wear footwear suitable for a farmhand to a Royal event."

"These boots have excellent arch support and you can't even see them under the dress," I mutter, but she's already continuing her lecture.

"This is precisely the sort of behavior I've been sent to correct. A proper duchess would be outside, offering condolences to the grieving, perhaps organizing a memorial fund. She would not be..." Mrs. Trechón gestures at the crime scene with a hand motion that somehow conveys both disgust and disappointment, "... doing whatever this is."

Jack bristles at Mrs. Trechón's tone. He hates the way she talks to me and has been itching to intervene, but I've told him to let me handle it– and to Jack's credit, he's trying. Beside him, Officer Basilier snorts. "Trust me, I've been trying to get her to stop meddling in investigations for more than a year. Won't work. You might as well give up now." Officer Basilier says the words with her usual brusqueness, but she offers me a wink afterwards that tells me she's on my side.

"Perhaps," Jack interrupts smoothly, stepping forward with diplomatic charm, "Mrs. Trechón, your expertise would be invaluable in managing the press situation outside."

Mrs. Trechón's eyes narrow slightly. She knows she's being managed, but Jack has given her an out that allows her to maintain her dignity.

"The press," Jack continues, his voice taking on a thoughtful quality that disguises a deeper annoyance, "will need careful handling. They'll want to know about the

Duchess's response, the official statement from the castle. Someone with your understanding of proper protocol would ensure the right message is conveyed. You could probably offer a statement better than Rebecca herself, given your long-term experience dealing with Royal trouble."

I watch Mrs. Trechón's face as she weighs her options. She could stay and continue lecturing me about proper duchess behavior, or she could go outside and control the narrative with the press— something she wants to do, deep down.

"*Très bien,*" she finally says, smoothing an imaginary wrinkle from her skirt. "I shall ensure the press receives appropriate information. But this conversation is not finished, Your Grace. We will discuss proper boundaries when you return to the castle."

She turns on her designer heel with military precision and clicks her way off the stage. I hear her muttering something in French that probably isn't complimentary, but at least she's heading for the exit.

Jack waits until the theater door closes behind her before turning back to us. "That should buy us some time."

"My hero," I say, and mean it.

"I wish I could get rid of her entirely for you," Jack shrugs, his face reddening. "If you'd only let me call my Aunt—"

"We have to handle this the way we discussed," I say, waving a hand in the air. Jack and I have talked about Mrs. Trechón at length, and we've agreed there's no point in angering the Queen so early in my duchessdom. Still, I can tell he feels helpless, and he'd like to tell Mrs. Trechón to take a hike.

"Her tone towards you is unacceptable," he says, shaking his head. "There are those in the noble families who treat the Royals like we can't live without them. I warned you this life meant madness, I'm afraid—"

"I'd rather be mad with you then sane with anyone else," I

say, looping my arm through Jack's and reaching up to kiss him.

"Ugh, horrific," Officer Basilier rolls her eyes at our embrace. "Forcing us all to witness your public affection. Bring back Mrs. Trechón," she jokingly calls over her shoulder. "She'll put a stop to it!"

"Hey," Maggie laughs. "They're in the honeymoon phase! Give them a break!"

"If I can ever get her to go on an actual honeymoon," Jack grumbles, rolling his eyes.

Jack's been trying to plan our honeymoon for weeks, but so far, my new royal duties— like the patronage at the theatre — have interrupted our plans. And now, there's a murder to solve, on top of everything.

"Fair enough," Officer Basilier agrees. "All kidding aside, Mrs. Trechón is a true nightmare, Rebecca. Let me know if you ever want me to use my stun gun on her," she says, patting the device on her belt. "I could make it look like an accident. As in, 'Oops, thought she was reaching for a weapon. That pearl necklace looked awfully threatening.'"

"Don't tempt me," I say, though we both know I'd never actually take her up on it. Probably. "Besides, the Queen would just send someone worse. She thinks I need the help because of the scandals in the press. At least Mrs. Trechón's predictable."

"Speaking of predictable," Officer Basilier says, her tone shifting to business as she pulls out a small notebook, "let's talk about our very unpredictable murder."

She gestures to the body, and we all move a bit closer, though Joe and Luma maintain their positions like the well-trained animals they are. The foam around Tom's mouth has dried slightly under the stage lights, giving his face an even more grotesque appearance.

"Victim is Tom Prink, age thirty-four. Local man, born and

raised in the village," Officer Basilier reads off her notepad. "His parents run the flower shop a few blocks past the town square. You know, the one with the window boxes that win the competition every year?"

I nod. I've bought arrangements there for the castle.

"This was his first major role," Officer Basilier continues, consulting her notes. "Playing Sly in *Taming of the Shrew*. According to the director— Jenny Jay, who's been surprisingly helpful despite being in the middle of what she calls 'an artistic catastrophe'— Tom was thrilled. He'd been doing community theater for years, small parts, chorus work. But Sly in a production from the Royal Theater Company? That was his big break."

"Sly's not exactly a huge part," Maggie points out. "He's only in the induction, isn't he? The drunk who gets tricked into thinking he's a lord?"

"Still bigger than Townsperson Number Three," Officer Basilier says. "And it's a named character with actual lines. In the theater world, that matters."

Jack moves slightly, and I can see him processing this information with that particular intensity he gets when something doesn't quite add up. "So someone killed him over a relatively minor role in a regional production?"

"That's what we need to figure out," Officer Basilier says. "Jenny's arranged for us to interview the cast and crew. She's actually got them organized in the green room with time slots and everything. Very efficient. She keeps saying things like 'the show must go on' and 'Tom would want us to continue,' but I can tell she's rattled."

"Who wouldn't be?" I ask, looking at poor Tom again. "Having someone die during your production— that's got to be a director's worst nightmare."

"Actually, she said her worst nightmare involves forgetting all the words to her acceptance speech at the International Arts Awards, but this is definitely top five,"

Officer Basilier says dryly. "Anyway, she's helped me compile a list of people with potential motives. There are a few interesting candidates, but one name really stands out."

She pauses for effect, and I know she's enjoying this bit of drama. Officer Basilier might act tough and by-the-book, but she loves a good reveal as much as anyone.

"We're particularly interested in *Brent Thoroughgood*."

Maggie lets out a gasp that's so sudden and loud that both dogs actually break their professional stillness to look at her.

"*The* Brent Thoroughgood?" she practically squeaks. "From '*L'Été at Sandcastle High*'? Oh my God, he was my teen crush! I had his poster on my wall. He played Rex Waterstone, the bad boy surfer who secretly wrote poetry. I must have watched that show a hundred times."

"Never seen it," I shrug. "But it sounds like the American TV Show *The O.C.*"

"That's the one," Officer Basilier confirms, though she looks slightly amused by Maggie's fangirl reaction. "Apparently his career didn't quite take off the way everyone expected after the show ended. He's done a few action movies that flopped. Since then, he's been in regional theater for the past few years, trying to prove he's a 'serious actor' now."

"He's *here*? In our production?" Maggie asks, her voice still pitched higher than normal. She hits my arm, making me yelp. "Rebecca, how come you didn't tell me?!"

"Sorry, I was busy figuring out how to be a Duchess," I say, rubbing my arm.

"Wait, who does he play?" Maggie asks, practically dripping with excitement.

"Petruchio," Officer Basilier says. "The male lead. The one who 'tames' Katherine."

"Of course he does," I mutter. "The bad boy grows up to play the ultimate bad boy role."

"But here's the interesting part," Officer Basilier continues, and I can tell from her tone that we're getting to the real revelation. "Jenny mentioned that Brent had some very specific requirements in his contract. Unusual ones."

"Like what?" Jack asks. "Special dietary needs? A specific brand of water in his dressing room?"

"Bigger than that," Officer Basilier says. "He insisted that his younger brother be cast in the production. Made it a deal-breaker. No brother, no Brent."

"That's nepotism," Maggie says, disappointed. Though she still looks a bit starry-eyed at the thought of her teen crush being in town.

"That's not even the interesting part," Officer Basilier says, and now she's got that look she gets when she's about to drop the real bombshell. "Seems nepotism only goes so far. Want to guess which role the brother got?"

We all look at each other, and I can feel the pieces starting to click into place even before she says it.

"Tom's understudy," I say, and it's not a question.

"Bingo," Officer Basilier confirms. "Josh Thoroughgood— Brent's little brother— was Tom Prink's understudy for the role of Sly."

The silence that follows is heavy with implication. Even Joe seems to sense the shift in mood, his ears perking up slightly.

"So Tom dies," Jack says slowly, "and the brother of the star gets promoted to the role."

"That's one hell of a coincidence," I say.

"I don't believe in coincidences when there's foam around someone's mouth," Officer Basilier says grimly.

Maggie looks devastated. "But... but Rex Waterstone would never..."

"Rex Waterstone was a character," Officer Basilier reminds her gently. "Brent Thoroughgood is a real person with a real motive."

We all look back at Tom's body, and suddenly the foam around his mouth seems less like a random tragedy and more like a very deliberate message.

Someone wanted Tom out of the way. And I'm going to find out who.

CHAPTER
Three

AS WE APPROACH the green room door, I can't help but think about the press outside, and wonder what the headlines will say about me tomorrow morning. "The Duchess of Death" has a certain ring to it, though Mrs. Trechón would probably faint at the nickname.

Jack pauses before we reach the door, pulling me aside. The hallway backstage is narrow, with exposed brick and framed playbills of past productions lining the walls.

"I'd better let the Royal Investigators do their work," he says with a soft smile, the one that still makes my heart do a little flip even after all we've been through together. "I'll leave you to it and go run interference with the press."

"And Mrs. Trechón," I add, unable to keep the dread from my voice. "She's probably out there right now, telling reporters about my unsuitable footwear choices and how a proper duchess would never solve murders."

"Leave her to me," Jack says, his eyes twinkling with mischief. "I'll keep her busy. I can buy you at least a couple hours."

He leans down and kisses me, a proper kiss that makes Maggie clear her throat and Officer Basilier mutter something about "public indecency." I don't care. I'm still not used to the fact that I can just kiss the Duke of Atwood whenever I want. That he's my husband.

"Come on, Joe," Jack says, turning to my enormous dog who's been sitting patiently at my heel. "You too, Luma."

The two dogs perk up at the sound of their names, and Jack clips leashes onto both their collars.

"Both of them?" I ask, a little nervous. Joe is usually my shadow.

Jack puts his hands in the air as if he's been caught. "Don't blame me!" He says, nodding at Officer Basilier. "It was her idea."

I stare at Officer Basilier, betrayed.

"My intel says Brent's little brother is allergic to dogs, Orange," Officer Basiler says gruffly. "Can't tell if he's a murderer in between sneezes."

"Fair enough," I agree, bending down to pat Joe's head. His soft fur is a familiar comfort under my hand. "Be good for Mommy!"

"Besides," Jack adds, "Joe is excellent at looking intimidating. Might keep Mrs. Trechón at a comfortable distance."

"Ooh, great idea!" I say, thrilled at the thought. "The training signal for growling is one hand in the air, fist closed." I demonstrate the move. Joe immediately crouches into an angry stance, his teeth bared, a horrific growl coming out of his mouth. Then, he returns to his usual happy face, tongue out, tail wagging.

"Alright, alright," Officer Basilier interrupts. "If you two are quite finished, we have a murder to solve."

Jack straightens up, instantly transforming from my affectionate husband back into the dignified Duke of Atwood. It's a switch I've seen him make countless times, and it never ceases to amaze me how effortlessly he moves between his personal and public personas.

"Good luck," he says, his voice carrying the weight of his title now. "I'll handle everything out front."

We watch as he walks away, the two dogs trotting obediently at his side. Joe glances back at me once, as if making sure I'll be okay without him, and I give him a little nod. He huffs what seems like a sigh and then continues following Jack.

"Ready?" Officer Basilier asks, her hand on the doorknob.

"As I'll ever be," I reply.

The green room of Monrovia's Royal Theatre lives up to its prestigious reputation. It's nothing like the cramped, fluorescent-lit spaces I've seen backstage at community theaters. This room is genuinely green— the walls are painted a soft sage that catches the light from an honest-to-goodness crystal chandelier hanging from the ceiling. Plush velvet couches in deep emerald are arranged in a conversational grouping, with gleaming mahogany side tables holding delicate porcelain tea services. The carpet underfoot is thick enough that our footsteps are muffled as we enter.

The room falls silent as we step inside. Five people are arranged on the couches, all turning to look at us with expressions ranging from curiosity to outright hostility.

"Everyone," Officer Basilier announces with an authoritative tone that makes it clear she's taking charge, "Thank you for your patience. I'm Officer Basilier of the Monrovian Police. With me are the Duchess of Atwood and Ms. Maggie Lefevere, both of whom serve as Royal Investigators. On behalf of the crown, they assist with investigations on occasion."

I try not to wince at the formal introduction. Being called "the Duchess of Atwood" still feels like she's talking about someone else.

A woman in a pleated skirt covered in tiny teapots springs to her feet. The skirt is paired with purple legwarmers and a bright yellow sweater that makes my eyes hurt a little.

"Your Grace!" she exclaims, rushing forward to grasp my

hand in both of hers. "So lovely to see you again, though under such tragic circumstances. I don't believe this is how either one of us saw the evening going—"

"Very true," I agree. "Maggie, Officer Basilier, this is Jenny Jay. We met at the patronage ceremony last month and have been keeping in touch off and on about the state of the Royal Theatre Company. She has an eye for the stage." *And skirts with outrageous patterns*, I think to myself but don't say it aloud.

"This is dreadful, just dreadful," Jenny continues, lowering her voice to what she probably thinks is a respectful volume but is actually still quite loud. "Poor Tom. But I know we'll get through this together."

Officer Basilier gently steers Jenny back toward the seating area. "If you don't mind, I'd like to make formal introductions for everyone."

Jenny nods and returns to her seat, smoothing her teapot skirt as she sits.

"As you know, this is Jenny Jay, the director of the production," Officer Basilier says, gesturing toward her. "Next to her is Monica Blanchart, who plays the leading female role in *Taming of the Shrew*, Katherina."

Monica barely looks up at the mention of her name. She's strikingly beautiful, with dark hair and eyes, but she seems to be trying to disappear into the couch cushions. Her hands are clasped tightly in her lap, and she offers the tiniest of nods in acknowledgment.

Despite Officer Basilier's statement that Monica plays the lead, I immediately recognize her as the woman who played the hostess in the opening. *The woman who held Tom as he died.*

As if she knows what I'm thinking, Officer Basilier adds, "Monica also played the hostess who passed Tom the cup. Is that correct, Ms. Blanchart?"

Monica nods, tears streaming out of her eyes. "I didn't know— I couldn't have known."

"Is it usual for an actor to play two roles?" Maggie pipes up, curious.

"We have a small cast," Jenny Jay interjects. "Many of our actors play more than one part."

Officer Basilier clears her throat, continuing: "Beside Ms. Blanchart is Brent Thoroughgood, who plays Petruchio."

Brent, unlike Monica, seems to expand to fill more space at the sound of his name. He's conventionally handsome in that "I was definitely the most popular boy in high school" way, with perfectly styled blonde hair and bright green eyes. He doesn't stand, but he does raise a hand in a lazy wave.

Beside me, I hear Maggie let out a little peep, but she stifles it under a cough.

"Pleasure," he drawls, his eyes moving over me in a way that makes me deeply uncomfortable. I recognize his accent as upper crust British. This is a man who comes from old stock, as they say, and his attitude— which seems to say he belongs anywhere— proves it. "Always delightful to meet a fan."

"I've actually never heard of you," I reply before I can stop myself.

Maggie nudges me sharply with her elbow, but Brent's smile only falters for a second before reappearing, slightly more forced.

"*I'm* a fan!" Maggie adds, practically jumping up and down. "I love sand," she rambles. "I love the show, I mean, I love *you*, I mean—"

I step on Maggie's foot gently, helping her avoid further mortification.

"Next to Mr. Thoroughgood is his brother, Josh Thoroughgood, who was Tom Prink's understudy," Officer Basilier continues smoothly.

Josh looks like a watered-down version of his brother— same features but somehow less defined, less memorable. He offers a nervous smile that doesn't reach his eyes.

"And finally, we have Cosmo Flap, the property master and stunt director for the production."

Cosmo is a plump man with gray hair and a dark mustache. He looks perpetually frazzled, as if he's just remembered he left the oven on at home.

"Now," Officer Basilier says, taking a seat in one of the few remaining chairs, "I know this is difficult, but I need to ask you all some questions about Tom Prink."

Maggie and I find seats of our own, and I notice that Maggie keeps sneaking glances at Brent, who either doesn't notice or pretends not to.

"Did Tom have any enemies that you know of?" Officer Basilier asks, her notebook ready. "Anyone who might have wished him harm?"

"Tom?" Jenny exclaims, her hands flying to her cheeks. "Enemies? Impossible! He was the sweetest man, always bringing coffee for everyone during early rehearsals. He volunteered to help build the sets on his days off. Everyone loved Tom."

"He was kind," Monica says, her voice so soft we all have to lean forward to hear her. "He helped me run lines when I was nervous. He never made me feel... *se sentir comme un poisson hors de l'eau*. Like a fish out of water." She lowers her eyes again, a blush creeping up her cheeks.

"The man was fine," Brent says with a shrug that seems deliberately casual. "A bit eager, maybe. Always trying to get me to go for drinks after rehearsal, asking for career advice. But harmless. Why exactly are we all here?" he continues, his tone sharpening. "I've got a call with my agent in twenty minutes. Some of us have international careers to maintain."

I watch Josh flinch slightly at his brother's words, and make a mental note of it. There's definitely some tension there.

"You're here," Officer Basilier says coolly, "because a man is dead, and all of you had access to the prop that killed him."

That silences the room again, the weight of her words settling over us like a heavy curtain.

"Tom was the nicest guy I've worked with in twenty years of theater, alright?" Cosmo adds after a moment, his voice carrying the weariness of someone who's seen it all. Like Brent, his accent sounds British to me, but not upper-crust. His cadence makes it clear he wasn't raised in Monrovia. "Always respected the props, never complained about costume fittings. A dream to work with, really."

"And now he's gone," Jenny says, her cheerful facade cracking just slightly. "Just terrible timing, too, with opening night ruined."

I catch Maggie's eye, and I can tell she's thinking the same thing I am: Jenny's concern about the show's timing seems a touch callous given the circumstances.

"Terrible timing for Tom, you mean," I say, watching Jenny's face carefully.

"Oh! Yes, of course," she backpedals quickly. "That's exactly what I meant. Terrible for Tom, primarily. Absolutely."

I'm not convinced, and from the way Officer Basilier's pen moves across her notebook, neither is she.

I lean forward, focusing on the prop master. From my years of animal training, I know that the most telling details often come from the people working behind the scenes, the ones who notice everything while others are busy performing. "Let's talk about the cup," I say to Cosmo. "The one Tom drank from. It was supposed to be a prop, right? With a certain liquid inside? Fake alcohol, like colored water?"

Cosmo's mustache twitches as all eyes turn to him. He pulls a handkerchief from his pocket and dabs at his forehead, though the room isn't particularly warm.

"Actually, no," he says, his voice carrying the exhaustion of someone who hasn't slept in days. "Tom specifically requested real wine for his part. Said it helped him get into character as a drunk. We used a new bottle every night."

"A new bottle?" Officer Basilier's pen hovers over her note-book. "Provided by whom?"

"The theater," Cosmo says. "We keep a small stock for special events and productions that require it. Nothing fancy, just basic red table wine."

"And who knew about this arrangement?" I ask.

Cosmo gestures vaguely around the room. "Everyone, I suppose. It wasn't a secret. Tom would joke about it during rehearsals. 'At least I get real booze for this part,' he'd say."

"Walk us through how the cup makes it to the stage," Officer Basilier prompts. "Specifically with the wine."

Cosmo sighs heavily, his shoulders slumping as if the weight of the entire production rests on them— which, from what I'm gathering, might not be far from the truth.

"I always open a new bottle about an hour before curtain. The way we practiced it in rehearsals, I pour it into Tom's pewter cup— the one he drinks from in the opening scene. I leave it on the prop table while I check the lighting cues with Jenny."

"You're the lighting director too?" Maggie asks, sounding surprised.

"No, no," Cosmo says, then pauses. "Well, yes, sort of. The actual lighting director quit last week— something about creative differences—" he glances quickly at Jenny, who suddenly becomes very interested in adjusting her teapot skirt, "—so I've been filling in. I'm also handling most of the wardrobe since our costume designer is only part-time."

"That's a lot of jobs," I observe.

Cosmo laughs, but there's no humor in it. "You have no idea. I'm property master, stunt coordinator, acting lighting director, assistant costume designer, and I've been helping with set changes because we're short-handed there too."

"And you're good at all of them," Jenny interjects, reaching over to pat his knee. "A true Renaissance man of the theater."

Cosmo's expression suggests he'd prefer to be a one-job

man with a reasonable workload, but he doesn't contradict her. Instead, he smiles at her, his eyes filled with admiration. "I want to help Jenny's vision come to life," he adds warmly, looking at her with a gentle gaze.

"So," Officer Basilier steers us back to the topic, "you left the cup on the prop table and went to check the lighting. Then what?"

"I was gone maybe fifteen minutes," Cosmo continues. "When I came back, I took the cup and placed it on the bar prop on stage— that's where Tom would pick it up during the performance. Then I had to rush to help Monica with a quick costume repair."

"A hook in the hostess costume came loose," Monica confirms softly. "It was nothing, really. I could have fixed it myself."

"So the cup was unattended twice," I summarize. "Once on the prop table and again on the stage."

"Pretty much," Cosmo agrees. "It's not usual protocol, but with everything I'm handling..." He trails off, spreading his hands in a gesture of helplessness.

"What about you, Monica?" Officer Basilier turns to Monica, who fidgets under her gaze. "You were alone with the cup on stage. Did you notice anything strange about the liquid inside before you handed it to Tom?"

Monica shakes her head. "No. It didn't smell strange. It didn't *look* strange. It was just… regular wine."

"We're testing the bottle and any remaining liquid," Officer Basilier says. "But it sounds like someone could have easily added something to the cup directly. Which means they got to the cup sometime between when the bottle was opened, and when the cup was placed on stage."

"I can't believe I'm the one who handed it to him," Monica says, her lower lip trembling. "I feel like *I* poisoned him. Like I'm responsible—"

"*Someone* poisoned him," Officer Basilier confirms. "Most likely, someone in this room."

"Officer Basilier!" Jenny exclaims, pressing a hand to her heart. "That's a terrible thing to say. Tom's death is tragic. Simply awful. But I assure you, Officer, no one on our team would have it in them to poison a man." She turns to me, her eyes wide and imploring. "Your Grace, I know this is a tragedy— a genuine tragedy— but I hope you'll consider allowing us to continue with the production."

I blink, caught off guard by the abrupt change of subject. "I'm not sure that's appropriate, given the circumstances—"

"Tom would have wanted the show to go on," Jenny insists, leaning forward so intensely I find myself leaning back to maintain personal space. "The theater was his life. And we have his understudy ready to step in." She gestures toward Josh, who looks like he'd rather be anywhere else right now.

"I'd need to consult with the police and the castle before making any decisions," I say carefully.

"Of course, of course," Jenny nods vigorously. "But as our Royal Patron, your support would mean everything. We could dedicate the performance to Tom's memory! A tribute to his talent and passion for the arts!"

I glance at Officer Basilier, who gives me a subtle shake of her head. We both know it's far too soon to be making these kinds of decisions.

"Let's focus on finding out what happened to Tom first," I say diplomatically.

"Absolutely right," Officer Basilier agrees. "And to do that, we need to understand everyone's movements last night. What about you, Mr. Thoroughgood?" Officer Basilier asks, turning to Brent. "The *elder* Mr. Thoroughgood," she clarifies when both brothers react.

Brent stretches his arms along the back of the couch, taking up even more space. "I was in my dressing room with my brother, going over his lines. Just in case, you know? Always good to be prepared."

"You were helping Josh prepare to be an understudy?" I ask, not bothering to hide my skepticism.

"Family first," Brent says with a smile that doesn't reach his eyes. "Besides, Josh gets nervous. Needed a pep talk."

Josh studies the floor, his ears reddening.

"Is that true, Josh?" Officer Basilier asks. He nods in response, but doesn't offer more.

"And what about you, Ms. Jay?" Officer Basilier continues.

"I was everywhere!" Jenny exclaims, throwing her hands up. "A director's work is never done. I was checking the house, making sure the programs were arranged properly, speaking with the lighting booth, giving last-minute notes to the ensemble. You can ask anyone—they all saw me rushing about."

Cosmo nods in confirmation. "Jenny's always running around before a show. It's why I have to handle so many other jobs."

I notice a flash of irritation cross Jenny's face at this comment, but it's quickly replaced by her usual enthusiastic expression.

"So to summarize," Officer Basilier says, "anyone could have accessed that cup during the time it was unattended."

"I suppose so," Cosmo admits reluctantly. "Though I can't imagine who would want to hurt Tom."

"Sometimes it's not about the victim," I say quietly. "Sometimes it's about what the victim's death makes possible for someone else."

A heavy silence falls over the room as my words sink in. Josh shifts uncomfortably in his seat, and I notice Brent's hand moving to his brother's shoulder in what appears to be a supportive gesture.

"It's a real bummer about Tom," Brent says, giving his brother's shoulder a squeeze. "Great guy, terrible loss. But the show will go on, right Jenny? And now Josh gets his shot at a real role. Silver lining and all that."

The casual way he says it sends a chill through me. Not quite grief or celebration, which might be less disturbing—just a pragmatic acknowledgment that his brother has benefited from Tom's death.

Josh looks mortified, but doesn't contradict his brother. Instead, he stares at his hands, shoulders hunched as if trying to make himself smaller.

"Opportunity born from tragedy," Officer Basilier murmurs, making another note in her book. "How convenient."

I catch her eye, and I know we're thinking the same thing: We've just found our prime suspect— or suspects.

CHAPTER

Four

THE SMELL of roast turkey hits me the moment I push open the door to our private dining room. It's a scent that doesn't belong in a Monrovian castle— it belongs in my childhood home in San Diego, where Thanksgiving meant my mother cursing at the oven while football blared from the living room. But here it is, wafting through the air of the Duke of Atwood's private dining room, because my husband asked Chef Renauld to make me feel at home. I'm still not used to having requests fulfilled like this, as if my random mentions of missing American comfort food are royal decrees.

"You're just in time," Jack says, rising from his seat at the head of our ornate mahogany table. He's changed out of the formal attire he wore to the theater and into what counts as casual for him— a light blue button-down and dark slacks.

"Sorry I'm late," I say, dropping a stack of manila folders onto the sideboard. "Officer Basilier sent over her notes from the interviews. I lost track of time reading them."

Jack smiles, but I catch the slight tightening around his eyes. "I assumed as much. You have that 'I'm solving a murder' furrow between your eyebrows."

I automatically touch the spot between my brows. "I don't have a murder-solving furrow."

"You absolutely do." Jack pulls out my chair. "Right there. It's quite adorable, actually. Your tell that you're deep in detective mode."

The dining room is smaller and more intimate than the grand state dining hall where we entertain official guests. This room, with its rich burgundy walls and gleaming silver candelabras, is where we eat when it's just us. Well, us and our fur babies. In the corner, Joe and Luma are already stationed at their respective dishes— Joe's silver, Luma's gold, because apparently even dog bowls have to follow royal protocol.

"Did Chef Renauld really make—" I start, but the answer arrives before I can finish the question.

Chef Renauld herself emerges from the adjoining butler's pantry, carrying a large, covered platter. Her crisp white uniform is immaculate as always, not a speck of food on it despite what must have been hours of cooking.

"Your Grace," she says with a slight nod to Jack, then turns to me. "Madame *Duchess*," Chef smiles at me. She still calls me Rebecca in private but uses my title teasingly when in a more formal setting. "I have prepared what I believe Americans call a 'Thanksgiving Dinner.' Though why one would want turkey and cranberry sauce at the same time, I cannot claim to know."

I bite back a smile. Chef Renauld's dry observations about American customs never fail to amuse me.

"It smells incredible," I tell her.

She lifts the cover from the platter with a flourish, revealing a perfectly roasted turkey surrounded by glazed sweet potatoes, bright orange cranberry sauce (not the jellied kind from a can that I secretly prefer), and some kind of fancy stuffing with nuts and dried fruits.

"I have taken certain... liberties," she says, her French

accent becoming more pronounced as she describes her food. "The cranberry has a hint of Monrovian orange liqueur. The stuffing includes our local chestnuts and the wild mushrooms from the eastern forest. And the turkey—," she pauses dramatically, "—is rubbed with herbs from my private garden."

"It looks amazing," I say, genuinely touched by the effort.

Chef Renauld sniffs slightly, but I can tell she's pleased. "It will do, I hope. The pumpkin pie cooling in the kitchen is better."

With that, she disappears back into the pantry, and I hear the discrete servant's door close behind her.

Jack reaches for the carving set. "Shall I?"

"Please," I say, laughing as he tries to carve the turkey. His effort is clumsy, and he almost knicks his thumb with the knife. As much as Jack tries to be an average guy, some moments make it clear he's had help most of his life.

"I don't think I've had Thanksgiving food before the actual holiday. Definitely not in the first week of November."

Jack freezes as if a terrible thought has occurred to him. "Have I botched it?" he says, looking sad. "Should we have waited until the actual day? Maybe you wanted to celebrate your American holiday here and I've planned it too early…"

My heart does a little flip. Even after several months of marriage, these thoughtful gestures still catch me off guard. How did I end up with this man who notices everything and tries so hard to make me happy?

"Jack," I laugh. "This is perfect. Don't worry."

He exhales in relief. "That's good because Chef Renauld would be quite upset with me if I requested something else. She was very much engaged in the challenge. She spent three days researching traditional recipes and then, naturally, deciding how to improve them."

I shake my head, smirking as Jack passes me my plate,

now topped with turkey and every manner of side dish. "Of course she did."

We settle into eating, the only sounds for a few minutes being the clink of silverware and the appreciative grunts from the corner where Joe and Luma are devouring their own special meals. Joe eats with the single-minded focus of a dog who spent his formative years wondering where his next meal would come from, despite the fact that he's never missed a feeding in his entire pampered life. Luma, in contrast, takes dainty bites, pausing occasionally to look around the room as if making sure her good manners are being properly appreciated. I'm always amazed by the way in which dogs fit their owners.

"Oh," Jack says suddenly, setting down his fork. "I almost forgot."

He reaches beneath his chair and pulls out a leather portfolio, which he places on the table between us. "I've been doing some research."

I take another bite of the sweet potatoes, which have been transformed into something magical by Chef Renauld's mysterious techniques. "Research on what?"

Jack flips open the portfolio, revealing glossy brochures featuring pristine beaches, snow-capped mountains, and luxurious resorts. "Honeymoon options."

"Oh," I say, trying to shift mental gears from murder suspects to vacation destinations. "Right. The honeymoon."

The honeymoon we should have taken immediately after our wedding three weeks ago?

"I've narrowed it down to a few choices," he continues, spreading the brochures out like a hand of cards. "The private island in the Maldives has excellent security protocols, which would allow us to truly relax. The château in the French Alps offers complete privacy and spectacular views. And the villa in Tuscany comes with its own vineyard and a staff that's been security-cleared by the Monrovian Royal Guard."

I nod, trying to focus on the pictures of paradise in front of me, but my mind keeps drifting back to the folders I brought home. To Tom Prink's foam-flecked mouth and the look of calculation in Brent Thoroughgood's eyes when he talked about his brother getting a bigger role.

"They all look wonderful," I say, reaching for my water glass. "Truly."

Jack's expression doesn't change, but I see a slight droop in his shoulders. "You're not really looking at them, are you?"

"I am!" I protest, pointing at a random brochure. "Look, that one has... water. Very blue water. Lovely."

"That's the Alps, Rebecca. Those are mountains."

"Right," I say, feeling a flush of embarrassment. "Mountains. Even better."

Jack sighs, not unkindly. "You're thinking about the murder."

It's not a question, so I don't bother denying it. "I can't help it," I admit. "I feel responsible. This was my first official patronage as Duchess. I was supposed to bring prestige to the Royal Theatre Company, not a homicide investigation."

"No one blames you for what happened," Jack says, reaching across the table to take my hand. His fingers are warm against mine.

"Mrs. Trechón does," I mutter. "She practically accused me of summoning death with my unsuitable footwear."

Jack laughs. "Mrs. Trechón would find fault with an angel descending from heaven if its wings weren't properly pressed."

I smile despite myself, but the momentary levity fades quickly. "I just keep thinking about Tom. About the fact that someone decided he shouldn't be alive anymore, and used *my* official event to make that happen."

Jack squeezes my hand before releasing it. "I understand." And he does, which is one of the countless reasons I love him. "These are just ideas for when you're ready. I've been dealing with Royal intrigue my entire life. You can't blame a man for wanting to get away."

I push my plate aside and reach for the folders I brought in. "Officer Basilier gave me her notes on all the suspects. She's narrowed it down to a few key people with real motives."

Jack watches me for a moment, then closes the honeymoon portfolio. He moves his plate aside too, making room for my investigative materials. "Alright, let's hear it."

I feel a rush of gratitude as I open the first folder. "So the primary suspects are Brent Thoroughgood and his brother, Josh. Brent insisted that Josh be cast as Tom's understudy as a condition of taking the lead role. Now, with Tom gone, Josh gets to play Sly."

"That's quite a convenient outcome for the brother," Jack observes, taking a sip of his wine.

"Exactly," I say, warming to my subject. "And get this— Officer Basilier did some digging. Turns out Josh has tried and failed to get cast in several productions around Monrovia in the last year. He's auditioned for at least three shows and never made it past callbacks."

"Not particularly talented?"

"Apparently not," I say, flipping through the pages. "But suddenly his brother gets some leverage, insists Josh be included, and boom— he's in. Then the person whose role he's understudying conveniently drops dead on opening night."

Jack leans forward, clearly intrigued despite himself. "Do you think Josh killed Tom to get the role?"

"Maybe," I say. "Or maybe Brent did it for him. From what I saw of their dynamic, Brent seems to be the type of older brother who 'fixes' things for his less capable sibling."

"Like poisoning an actor so his brother can have a minor role in a regional production?" Jack raises an eyebrow. "That seems rather extreme."

"It does," I agree. "But there's more. Officer Basilier found out that Brent's career isn't doing as well as he wants everyone to believe. That TV show he was on ended over a decade ago, followed by a few action movies that flopped. This production was supposed to be his big comeback, prove he's a serious actor now."

"And how does killing Tom Prink help with that?"

I shuffle through more papers. "That's what I'm still figuring out. But it could be about controlling the narrative. Maybe Tom knew something about Brent that could damage his reputation further? Or maybe it's even simpler— maybe Brent is just helping his brother get a foot in the door of professional acting."

"Murder seems like an awfully big step to get your brother a small role," Jack points out.

"True," I concede. "But people have killed for less. And there's something about the way Brent talked about Tom's death, so casual and calculating. Like it was just a casting change, not a tragedy."

Joe lets out a loud burp from his corner, briefly distracting us both. He looks supremely satisfied with himself, while Luma gives him what can only be described as a judgmental side-eye.

"What about the other suspects?" Jack asks, returning to the conversation.

I pull out another folder. "Jenny Jay, the director. She's been struggling to keep this production together. They've lost several key staff members in recent weeks— lighting designer, costume designer— and she's been forcing Cosmo, the prop master, to pick up the slack. Tom's death creates a big problem for her production, but she's also bizarrely focused on making sure the show goes on."

"That could just be the mentality of theater people," Jack suggests. "The show must go on and all that."

"Maybe," I say, unconvinced. "But she was way too interested in securing my permission to continue with the production, considering one of her actors had just been murdered. Almost like she was worried about something beyond just the show being canceled."

I continue flipping through papers, so engrossed in the details of the case that I almost miss Jack's small sigh. Almost, but not quite. I look up to find him watching me with a mixture of fondness and resignation.

"I guess the honeymoon will have to wait," he says softly. "Until this is solved."

"What?" I blink, momentarily confused. Then I see the closed portfolio of brochures, pushed to the side of the table, and realize what I've been doing. Again. Putting the case ahead of our plans. "Oh, Jack, no—we can still go on the honeymoon. I just need to figure this out first, and then—"

He smiles, but it doesn't quite reach his eyes. "It's alright, Rebecca. I understand. This is important to you, and it should be. You're right to take it seriously."

"But our honeymoon is important too," I say, feeling a stab of guilt.

"It is," he agrees. "And it will happen. When the time is right. For now… you've got a murder to solve."

He reaches for my hand and squeezes it gently, offering a diplomatic smile that carries nothing but warmth within it. His face says he's fine with prioritizing the solving of this case over a romantic getaway, but his eyes tell a different story.

Tell him you'll drop the case and leave tomorrow, I think, shaking my head at how dumb I can be sometimes.

I *should* just go away on my honeymoon. But to leave now feels like letting Mrs. Trechón win. And it's not just her. An entire country is waiting for me to fail at being a duchess. Somehow, solving this case means more than just bringing justice. It means proving to everyone I can be my true self— Rebecca Orange, animal trainer, Royal Investigator, ugly-boot-wearer— *and* a Duchess. If I don't prove myself now, I'll never get the chance.

"Are you sure you're okay waiting?"

"Definitely," Jack says. His fork scrapes the plate, and even though the conversation is over, the weight of what's unsaid still clings to the air.

CHAPTER
Five

CAFÉ DE FLORE feels like a sanctuary this morning. The aroma of fresh pastries and coffee wraps around me like a hug as I push open the door, Joe trotting faithfully at my heel. After a night of murder, mysterious suspects, and marriage guilt, I need the comfort of caffeine and carbs more than I need oxygen. I spot Maggie already waiting at our usual corner table, her blonde braids nearly glowing in the morning sunlight streaming through the window. She waves with enthusiasm that should be illegal before 9 a.m.

"There she is!" Maggie calls out. "The Duchess of... what's the coffee version of Atwood? The Duchess of Caffeinewood?"

"Just Orange is fine this morning," I mutter, sliding into the chair across from her. "Or better yet, just Rebecca. I've had enough of titles and protocol for one lifetime, and it's not even 9 o'clock."

Joe, sensing we're settling in, plops down beside my chair with a dramatic sigh. His eyes immediately lock onto Jocelyn, the café's owner, who's arranging fresh flowers on the counter. Joe knows exactly who controls the treat supply chain in this establishment.

"Bad night?" Maggie asks, studying my face with concern.

"Let's just say that discussing honeymoon plans over turkey dinner while simultaneously reviewing murder suspects isn't the romantic evening Jack had in mind." I rub my temples, where a dull headache is forming. "I'm pretty sure I fell asleep mid-sentence talking about the Alps. Or possibly the Maldives."

"Oh, Becs," Maggie winces. "The famous honeymoon planning session finally happened?"

"It happened. It crashed. It burned." I sigh. "I'm officially the worst wife in Monrovian history. Is there a dungeon for duchesses who can't prioritize their marriage over murder investigations?"

Maggie reaches across the table and pats my hand. "If there is, I'll bring you pastries. Daily."

The soft tinkling of the bell above the door announces another customer, but Joe's sudden alertness tells me before I turn around that Jocelyn has spotted us. She emerges from behind the counter, her kind face brightening as she approaches our table.

"Good morning, ladies!" she says warmly, her voice soft but clear. "And good morning to you too, magnificent beast." She bends slightly to offer Joe her hand, which he sniffs politely before giving it a gentle lick of approval.

"Morning, Jocelyn," I reply. "We need the strongest, sweetest, most decadent breakfast you can legally serve us. Preferably with caffeine levels that would make a medical professional concerned."

Jocelyn laughs, the sound like wind chimes. "I have just the thing. The pumpkin-cinnamon lattes are fresh, and I just pulled ham and swiss croissants from the oven. And for this handsome gentleman..." She gives Joe an affectionate scratch behind his ears. "I have a special cinnamon bone I've been saving. Perfect for a distinguished palace dog."

Joe's tail thumps against the floor with such force I'm

surprised it doesn't shake the building. His eyes grow round and pleading, as if to say, "You see? This is why I love this place. This woman understands my worth."

"That sounds perfect," I tell her. "And can we get it all to go? We've got a full morning ahead."

"Investigating?" Jocelyn asks, her eyes widening slightly. She leans in, lowering her voice. "About poor Tom?"

Maggie nods. "We're meeting with suspects while Officer Basilier runs tests on the poison sample from the wine bottle."

"Such a terrible thing," Jocelyn shakes her head, her expression genuinely sad. "Tom came in here almost every morning. Always ordered the same thing— black coffee and an almond croissant. He'd sit by the window and run his lines." She sighs. "Hard to believe he's gone."

"Did he ever come in with any of the cast or crew?" I ask, my investigator instincts immediately activating.

"Sometimes with that quiet girl, Monica. They'd sit for hours, just talking. She seemed sweet on him, if you ask me." Jocelyn pauses, considering. "And occasionally with that prop fellow— Cosmo? He and Tom would argue about staging or something theatrical. Never seemed serious, though."

I file this information away. Connections I hadn't known about— Monica and Tom spending time together outside rehearsal, Cosmo and Tom having professional disagreements. It could mean something. Or nothing.

"Well, it's good you're looking into it," Jocelyn says, straightening up. "Especially after how bad the press was this morning."

I freeze mid-reach for my water glass. "What press?"

Jocelyn's face falls. "Oh dear. You haven't seen? The papers... they're not being very kind about what happened. About your patronage."

My stomach drops faster than an elevator with cut cables. "No, I came straight here from the castle. I haven't seen anything."

Jocelyn and Maggie exchange a look that sends alarm bells ringing through my head.

"How bad is it?" I ask.

"Well..." Maggie starts, then hesitates.

"They're calling you things," Jocelyn says gently. "Terrible nicknames. Making it sound like trouble follows you. Like you're... bad luck."

"They're saying I'm cursed?" I ask, my voice rising. "Because one man was murdered at my first patronage event? That's hardly a pattern!"

Though if I'm being honest with myself, this isn't the first dead body I've encountered since coming to Monrovia. Or even the second. But you'd think solving the murders might at least make up for the fact they seem to follow me!

"I'll get your order ready," Jocelyn says, clearly wanting to escape this uncomfortable conversation. She hurries back to the counter, leaving me to process this new information.

"Were you planning to tell me about this?" I ask Maggie, who has suddenly become very interested in a spot on the tablecloth.

"I was going to ease you into it," she admits. "After coffee. And maybe a tranquilizer."

"That bad?"

"Let's just say Mrs. Trechón is going to have a field day with this one."

I groan and let my head drop into my hands. "Perfect. Just what I need. More ammunition for her 'proper duchesses don't attract murderers' lectures."

Jocelyn returns with a to-go bag and two large cups in a cardboard carrier. She places them on the table with a sympathetic smile. "Don't you worry about those papers," she says firmly. "People around here know you. They know you're trying to help."

"Thanks, Jocelyn," I say, managing a small smile.

"And here," she adds, producing a large, twisted bone-shaped treat that smells strongly of cinnamon. "For the handsome investigator."

Joe sits up so straight he practically levitates. I take the bone and hold it for a moment, making him wait. "Gentle," I remind him, and he takes it from my hand with exaggerated care before immediately retreating under the table to enjoy his treasure.

"We'd better get moving," Maggie says, collecting our to-go order. "We've got a full day of suspect interviews ahead of us."

I nod, standing up and giving Jocelyn a grateful smile. "Thanks for everything."

"Anytime," she says. "And Rebecca? Don't let them get to you. You'll sort this out. You always do."

Her confidence in me is touching, but as I tug gently on Joe's leash to get him out from under the table, I can't help but wonder if she's right. The press is turning against me, my husband is disappointed I won't go on holiday with him, and Mrs. Trechón is probably preparing a lecture on how proper duchesses don't have their names splashed across headlines alongside the word "death."

"Ready to face the music?" Maggie asks as we reach the door.

"No," I admit. "But let's do it anyway. First stop, the newsstand. I need to see exactly what we're dealing with."

Joe, cinnamon bone clamped firmly between his jaws, trots beside me with blissful ignorance of the public relations disaster awaiting us. At least someone's having a good morning.

———

The newsstand sits at the edge of the town square, strategically positioned to catch both tourists heading to gawk at royal architecture and locals going about their daily business. It's a charming little structure, with a red-tiled roof and walls covered in ivy that's been carefully trimmed around the display windows. Right now, though, it might as well be the gates of hell, considering what horrors await me on those pristinely arranged newspaper racks. My coffee suddenly feels inadequate for the task ahead.

"Maybe it's not that bad," I mutter, more to myself than to Maggie. "Maybe Jocelyn was exaggerating."

Maggie makes a noncommittal noise that does nothing for my confidence. Joe, still happily working on his cinnamon bone, remains the only one of us blissfully unaware of my impending public relations nightmare.

As we approach, I spot Zacharia, Rodrigo's former apprentice who now runs the newsstand. He's arranging magazines with the precision of someone setting up dominoes, his skinny frame leaning over the counter with intense concentration. When he notices us, his eyes widen, and he straightens up so quickly I'm worried he might have given himself whiplash.

"Rebecca!" he exclaims, his voice cracking slightly. "I mean, Your Grace! Good morning! I, uh—" He glances nervously at the front pages displayed behind him, then back at me. "I went with the nicest headline I could! Honest! The other publications weren't nearly as... considerate."

Great. Even the newsstand guy is pitying me. This day is off to a spectacular start.

"Let's see it, Zacharia," I say, steeling myself. "All of it."

He hesitates, then steps aside with the reluctance of someone revealing a particularly embarrassing stain.

The headlines hit me like a physical blow. They're worse than I imagined.

"*DUCHESS OF DEATH STRIKES AGAIN!*" screams the *Monrovian Daily* in bold red letters above a photo of me looking confused outside the theater last night. The subtitle adds: "Royal Patronage Turns Deadly as Actor Dies on Stage."

Next to it, the *Atwood Chronicle* proclaims: "*MURDER MOST ROYAL*: Duchess's Theater Debut Ends in Tragedy." They've used a photo where I appear to be smirking, though I'm pretty sure I was just trying not to sneeze.

The tabloid *Monrovian Mirror*, never one for subtlety, has gone with: "*THE CURSE OF ORANGE*: Is the New Duchess Bringing Bad Luck to the Royal Family?" Complete with a montage of every crime scene I've been associated with since arriving in Monrovia.

"Oh my God," I whisper, the coffee in my stomach turning to acid.

"I know, it's terrible," Zacharia says, fidgeting with the sleeve of his shirt. "But look at mine!" He reaches under the counter and proudly produces a magazine— *The Monrovian Messenger*, Rodrigo's old publication that Zacharia now runs.

He holds it up like it's a shield against my potential wrath. The headline reads: "*ORANGE YOU GLAD YOU DIDN'T SEE THE SHOW LAST NIGHT?*" accompanied by a relatively decent photo of me entering the theater with Jack.

I stare at him, processing the horrible pun on my last name. He stares back, a hopeful smile twitching on his lips.

"That's... better?" I manage, not entirely sure if it is.

"I made sure we weren't as mean as the others!" Zacharia insists. "Our article focuses more on the production itself and how the Royal Theatre Company will move forward. I even included a nice quote from your husband about your dedication to the arts."

"Jack gave a quote?" I ask, surprised.

"This morning. He called every publication personally," Maggie says, giving my arm a supportive squeeze. "Some just chose not to use it."

I'm touched by Jack's effort, even as I'm horrified by the rest of the coverage. I should have expected this. The press has been waiting for me to fail at being a duchess since the day Jack and I announced our engagement. A murder at my first official patronage event is like throwing raw meat to sharks.

"Can I get a copy of each?" I ask Zacharia, reaching for my wallet.

"Oh no, please," he says, quickly gathering the papers and rolling them together. "On the house. It's the least I can do." He pauses, then adds eagerly: "Also, if you happen to solve this case and want to give an exclusive interview afterward, *The Messenger* would be honored to—"

"Zacharia," I cut him off gently.

"Too soon?" He winces.

"Just a bit," I confirm, taking the rolled-up papers from him. "But I appreciate the thought. And the... less awful headline."

He beams at this minimal praise. "I tried! Rodrigo always said a good headline should make you laugh, not just shock you."

I nod, not trusting myself to comment further on Rodrigo's journalistic philosophy. Somehow, I doubt "ORANGE YOU GLAD" would have passed his standards, but Zacharia's heart is in the right place.

"We should get going," Maggie says, checking her watch. "Our appointment with Jenny is in twenty minutes."

"Right," I say, tucking the papers under my arm. "Thanks, Zacharia."

As we walk away from the newsstand, I can feel my initial shock hardening into determination. "They want to call me the 'Duchess of Death'? Fine. But they're going to eat those words when I solve this case."

"That's the spirit," Maggie says. "We'll turn this around. By the time we're done, they'll be calling you the 'Duchess of Justice' or something equally impressive."

"I'd settle for just 'Duchess' without any morbid adjectives attached," I mutter, but I'm starting to feel that familiar fire in my belly— the one that sparks whenever someone tells me I can't do something.

Joe finishes his bone with a final satisfying crunch and looks up at me expectantly, as if to say, "What's next, Mom?" He licks my hand, his tongue almost the size of my arm.

"We're going to solve this, Joe," I tell him. "We're going to find out who killed Tom Prink, and we're going to make the front pages for all the right reasons."

Joe wags his tail, thumping it against my leg in what I choose to interpret as wholehearted agreement. The weight of it almost knocks me over.

"Oh, and Rebecca?" Maggie says, her tone suddenly cautious. "I should probably mention... I may have promised Mrs. Trechón you'd meet with her this afternoon."

I stop walking so abruptly that Joe bumps into the back of my legs. "You what?"

Maggie holds up her hands defensively. "It was the only way I could convince her to let you out of the castle this morning! She wanted to do an emergency etiquette session on 'How Duchesses Handle Public Relations Crises.' I told her you'd be available after our interviews with suspects."

I groan. "So my options were either no investigation time or a lecture from the Duchess Police later? Great. Fantastic."

"Look at it this way," Maggie says, trying to sound optimistic. "By the time you see her, maybe we'll have solved the case and you can rub it in her face. Politely, of course. With proper duchess posture."

"Fine," I say. "I will handle it with the grace of a *Royal*."

Maggie smirks at my emphasis of the word "Royal." As we head toward the Theatre, I straighten my shoulders and lift my chin— not because Mrs. Trechón has been drilling proper posture into me for weeks, but because I'm Rebecca Orange, animal trainer turned Royal Investigator turned reluctant duchess. And if there's one thing I know how to do, it's solve a mystery, no matter what the press— or anyone else — thinks of me.

CHAPTER
Six

THE ATWOOD ROYAL Theatre smells like floor polish and chemical cleaner when we push through the heavy back door. The smell is so normal it's offensive– almost as if cleaning the space is an injustice to the murder that happened here only days ago. The show, apparently, must go on. Whether I approve it or not.

"Did we get the time wrong?" I whisper to Maggie as we navigate the dimly lit corridor behind the stage. Joe pads silently beside me, his massive paws making no sound on the worn carpet. "I thought the theater would be... I don't know, closed? Out of respect?"

Maggie shakes her head, checking her phone. "Jenny specifically said ten o'clock. And that's definitely hammering I hear."

She's right. The distant sound of construction echoes through the hallway— the rhythmic pounding of what must be a hammer on wood, the whir of an electric drill. As we get closer to the stage, voices drift toward us— someone projecting lines with theatrical flourish, another responding with equal dramatic intensity.

"Unbelievable," I mutter, clutching my coffee cup tighter. "Someone died here just days ago!"

We reach the wings of the stage, and I stop short at the sight before me. The stage is fully lit, the set for what must be Petruchio's house partially constructed. Monica and Brent stand center stage, facing each other with the intensity of two predators circling for a kill. Monica looks different than she did in the green room yesterday— gone is the shy, nervous woman who could barely meet our eyes. In her place stands Katherina, fierce and defiant, her voice carrying to the back of the empty theater.

"This is not the way to win a woman's love," she declares, her accent slipping into something more refined than her usual soft tones.

"Why, there's a wench!" Brent responds, his voice dripping with condescension as he circles her. "Come on and kiss me, Kate."

Above them, Cosmo hangs precariously from a rope system, slowly lowering what appears to be a decorative chandelier. His face is a mask of concentration as he carefully guides the set piece into position. He doesn't even glance our way, too focused on his task.

"What is happening right now?" I whisper to Maggie, who looks as stunned as I feel. "Are they seriously *rehearsing*?"

"Your Grace!"

The voice makes me jump. Jenny Jay appears seemingly from nowhere, today sporting a pleated skirt covered in tiny dinosaurs paired with bright orange legwarmers. The combination is somehow even more visually assaulting than yesterday's ensemble.

"I'm so glad you're here," she says, her voice pitched low but still managing to sound like she's announcing a prize winner. "As you can see, we're keeping the momentum going."

"I can see that," I reply, unable to keep the disbelief from my voice. "What I don't understand is why."

Jenny's smile flickers for just a moment before returning at full wattage. "Perhaps we could discuss this in my office? We're at a rather crucial point in the rehearsal, and I'd hate to interrupt the actors' flow."

On stage, Brent grabs Monica's wrist, pulling her closer in a move that looks a little too forceful for comfort. Monica doesn't break character, though I notice her eyes dart briefly toward us in the wings.

"Fine," I agree, though every instinct tells me to march onto that stage and shut this whole production down. "Lead the way."

Jenny clasps her hands together in what looks like relief and gestures for us to follow her. As we move away from the stage, I hear Monica's voice rise in a passionate delivery of Katherina's defiance against Petruchio's attempts to "tame" her. The irony isn't lost on me— a woman fighting against being controlled by a man who thinks he knows what's best for her, while I'm battling Mrs. Trechón and an entire society's expectations of how a duchess should behave.

Jenny's office is tucked away in a corner of the backstage area, a small room that feels even smaller due to the sheer volume of theatrical paraphernalia crammed into it. Every wall is plastered with posters from productions— some faded with age, others bright and new. They overlap like patches on a well-worn quilt, creating a dizzy visual timeline of Jenny's career.

"Please, sit," she says, clearing a stack of scripts from a pair of chairs facing her cluttered desk. There's nowhere for Joe to sit comfortably, so he settles for lying across the threshold of the open door, effectively blocking anyone from entering or leaving without stepping over 250 pounds of Tibetan Mastiff.

"Jenny," I begin, once Maggie and I are seated, "I have to

ask— what exactly do you think you're doing? A man was murdered on your stage less than a week ago."

Jenny's expression shifts to something approximating solemnity, though it doesn't quite reach her eyes. "I know, Your Grace. It's a tragedy beyond words. Poor Tom was... was..." She seems to struggle to find a suitable descriptor. "He was an integral part of our company."

"So integral that you've already replaced him and resumed rehearsals?" Maggie asks, her usually cheerful tone edged with disbelief.

Jenny has the grace to look at least somewhat embarrassed. "I understand how this must appear," she says, smoothing her dinosaur skirt. "But there are considerations that perhaps you haven't... well, there are practical matters at play. You see, this production represents a significant opportunity for all of us. With your patronage, Your Grace, we've been given a chance that many of us have waited our entire careers for."

She gestures to the wall of posters behind her. I take a closer look and notice something I missed at first glance— they're all for small, local productions. Community theater in tiny venues, school performances, productions in church basements and community centers. Nothing even approaching the scale or prestige of the Royal Theatre.

"This is your first major production," I confirm.

"Yes!" Jenny says, leaning forward eagerly. "Twenty-five years I've been directing, Your Grace. Twenty-five years of begging for funding, scrounging for rehearsal space, casting actors who can barely remember their lines because they're the only ones who showed up to audition." Her voice takes on a fervent quality that's almost religious in its intensity. "And finally, finally, I have a real budget, real actors, a real theater!"

I glance at Maggie, who raises an eyebrow ever so slightly. Jenny's passion is evident, but there's something unsettling about her prioritization.

"I understand this is important to you," I say carefully, "but a man died, Jenny. Tom was murdered. Doesn't that concern you more than the show?"

"Of course it does!" she insists, pressing a hand to her heart. "It's devastating. Absolutely devastating. But..." She hesitates, looking between Maggie and me as if gauging whether she can be honest. "But Tom would have wanted the show to go on. That's what they always say in theater, isn't it? The show must go on."

"I'm not sure that applies to murder," Maggie mutters.

"Let's back up," I suggest, trying to redirect the conversation. "We came here to ask you some questions about Tom and what happened that night. Maybe we could focus on that first?"

"Yes, of course," Jenny says, straightening in her chair. "Anything to help. Though I do hope that by the end of our conversation, you might reconsider allowing the production to continue. With appropriate memorials and tributes to Tom, naturally."

I resist the urge to roll my eyes. "Naturally. So, tell me about Tom's relationship with the other actors. Was there any tension between him and anyone in particular?"

Jenny shakes her head emphatically. "None whatsoever. Tom was universally beloved. A bit overeager at times, perhaps. He would often suggest changes to the blocking or delivery that weren't... well, they weren't always helpful. But that's just the enthusiasm of someone new to professional theater."

"What about his relationship with Josh Thoroughgood?" Maggie asks. "Tom must have known Josh was only cast because Brent insisted on it."

Something flickers across Jenny's face— annoyance, perhaps. "That arrangement was... unfortunate but necessary. Brent Thoroughgood brings name recognition to our production. Having a star in the lead role attracts audiences and sponsors. If the price of that was casting his less talented brother in a minor role as a mere understudy, it seemed a reasonable compromise."

"Did Tom see it that way?" I press.

Jenny hesitates. "He was professional about it. Though there may have been some... comments made during early rehearsals."

"What kind of comments?"

"Oh, nothing serious," Jenny says, waving a hand dismissively. "Just some gentle ribbing about Josh's difficulty with the lines. Josh can't remember a line to save his life, and in the odd moments where he had to substitute for Tom, he failed spectacularly. Tom offered to help him, actually. Very generous of him."

I make a mental note to ask Josh about these "gentle" comments. Something tells me Tom's version of helpful might have felt like something else entirely to someone struggling to keep up.

"What about you, Jenny?" I ask, changing tack. "How well did you know Tom outside of rehearsals?"

"Me?" She looks surprised by the question. "Oh, we didn't socialize, if that's what you're asking. Our relationship was strictly professional. Director and actor."

"So you wouldn't have any reason to want him gone?" Maggie asks bluntly.

Jenny's eyes widen. "Me? Good heavens, no! Tom's death is a catastrophe for this production! We've had to completely reconfigure everything with Josh stepping in. Cosmo's been working day and night to adjust the lighting cues, the program needs to be reprinted, press releases rewritten—" She stops suddenly, perhaps realizing how mercenary this all sounds.

"Speaking of programs," I say, "Jocelyn at *Café de Flore* mentioned you've already got Cosmo designing new ones?"

Jenny's cheeks flush slightly. "Well, yes. We need to be

prepared if— when— you give us permission to proceed. Time is of the essence in theater."

"It seems like Cosmo has a lot on his plate," I observe. "Lighting, props, stunts, and now programs too?"

"Cosmo is extremely capable," Jenny says quickly. "He's been my right hand for years. I don't know what I'd do without him."

"He seems very dedicated to you," Maggie notes.

Jenny smiles, a genuine expression that softens her features. "We've been through a lot together. The theater world isn't always kind, especially to directors without formal training or connections. Cosmo has stuck with me through productions where we couldn't afford to pay anyone, where we performed in unheated warehouses in the dead of winter. His loyalty is... well, it's irreplaceable."

For a moment, I glimpse something vulnerable beneath Jenny's aggressive enthusiasm— the uncertainty of someone who's spent decades chasing a dream that's always remained just out of reach.

But the moment passes quickly as she leans forward, her eyes suddenly alight with calculation. "Your Grace, I don't mean to be insensitive, but have you seen the papers this morning?"

My stomach tightens. "I have."

"Then you know they're being rather... unfair to you. Calling you the 'Duchess of Death' and such nonsense." She shakes her head as if deeply offended on my behalf. Then, she leans in as if she's about to deliver a pitch she's practiced many times in front of a mirror. "But what if we could change that narrative? What if, instead of the duchess whose patronage ended in tragedy, *you* became the duchess who refused to let tragedy stop the arts?"

I stare at her, not quite believing what I'm hearing.

"Think about it," Jenny continues, warming to her theme. "We dedicate the production to Tom. We give interviews about how you insisted the show must continue as a tribute to his talent. We turn this horrible situation into something positive— a statement about resilience, about the healing power of theater!"

"And coincidentally pack the house every night because of the publicity," I say dryly.

Jenny doesn't even have the decency to look embarrassed. In fact, she leans back as if she's pleased I understand what she's saying. "Well, yes! There would likely be increased interest. People are naturally curious about these things. In a strange way, this could be the best thing that could have happened for the production."

Beside me, Maggie makes a choking sound. Before she can interject, I say what we're both thinking. "The best thing? A man is dead, Jenny."

"I didn't mean—" she backtracks quickly. "That came out wrong. Of course Tom's death is tragic. Devastating. What I meant was that from this tragedy, something positive could emerge. For everyone involved. The actors get exposure, the theater gets attention, and you..." She points at me with enthusiasm that makes me lean back in my chair. "You get to reshape your public image!"

Joe, sensing my discomfort, lets out a low rumble from his position by the door. Not quite a growl, but a clear indication that he's paying attention and doesn't particularly like what he's hearing.

Jenny eyes him nervously. "The dog is quite... large, isn't he?"

"He is," I agree, not offering any reassurance. "And he's very protective."

Before Jenny can respond, there's a knock at the door. Joe lifts his massive head, then shifts his bulk just enough to allow someone to peek in without actually entering. It's Cosmo, his forehead glistening with sweat, his mustache slightly askew.

"Sorry to interrupt," he says, his eyes darting between us. "But Brent and Monica are ready to move on to the next scene. They're asking for your input on the blocking for the wedding."

"The wedding scene?" Jenny jumps to her feet, her face lighting up with renewed enthusiasm. "Perfect timing! Your Grace, perhaps you'd like to observe? It might help you understand the artistic significance of this production."

"I think we've seen enough for now," I say, rising from my chair. Joe immediately stands, alert and ready to go. "Maggie and I have other interviews to conduct this morning."

"Of course, of course," Jenny says, though disappointment is evident in her voice. "But you'll consider what I've said? About allowing the show to continue?"

I exchange a look with Maggie, who gives me the slightest shake of her head. "I'll take everything into consideration," I say noncommittally.

As Cosmo holds the door for us, I notice the exhaustion etched into his face, the slight tremor in his hand as he grips the doorframe. This man is running on fumes, carrying the weight of half a dozen jobs while Jenny pursues her dream of theatrical legitimacy.

"Thank you for your time, Jenny," I say as we prepare to leave. "We'll be in touch."

"Wonderful!" she chirps, following us to the door. "And do remember— dozens of jobs depend on this production. The costume makers, the set builders, the ticket takers... So many livelihoods hanging in the balance."

Her final attempt at emotional manipulation follows us down the hallway as we exit her office, Joe trotting between us like a furry bodyguard.

"Well," Maggie says once we're safely out of earshot. "That was..."

"Disturbing?" I suggest. "Calculating? Borderline ghoulish?"

"I was going to say 'revealing,' but those work too." Maggie shakes her head. "She really thinks Tom's murder could boost ticket sales."

"And reshape my public image," I add. "Don't forget that little bonus."

As we make our way back toward the stage, I can't help but wonder if Jenny's ruthless ambition extends beyond exploiting a tragedy for publicity. Could it have driven her to create the tragedy in the first place?

The sound of hammering grows louder, and somewhere in the theater, Brent's voice booms out a line about taming a shrew. The show, as they say, must go on. The question is: at what cost? And more importantly— who paid it with their life?

CHAPTER
Seven

THE CASTLE GATES loom ahead of us like the entrance to a medieval torture chamber— which, considering my upcoming appointment with Mrs. Trechón, isn't far from the truth. Joe trots faithfully beside me, blissfully unaware that while he gets to nap in a sunbeam somewhere, I'll be subjected to another excruciating lesson on how to be a proper duchess. Maggie walks on my other side, suspiciously avoiding eye contact.

"It's time, isn't it?" I say dramatically, acting as if I'm being shipped off to exile.

Maggie sighs, finally looking me in the eye. "Yes, I'm afraid it's time. You have a Duchess lesson scheduled for 10:30. In the Grand Ballroom."

I check my watch. It's already 10:15. "She'll tell me that fifteen minutes early is late in Duchess time." I sigh, looking longingly at the castle gates. "So while I'm practicing how to curtsy without breaking my spine, you'll be—what? Continuing the investigation without me?"

Maggie nods, looking guilty as she pulls out her notebook. "I'm going to write down everything we know so far. Try to make some sense of it all."

I groan, torn between my desire to solve Tom's murder and my obligation to at least attempt being a passable duchess. "Fine. But don't solve the case without me, please."

"Already planning on it." Maggie grins, then glances at Joe, who's watching our exchange with his head tilted in a way that makes him look simultaneously wise and confused. "What about Joe? Is he joining your duchess training or should I drop him off in the Royal Suite?"

I look down at my furry companion. Mrs. Trechón and Joe have a complicated relationship. She thinks he's undignified and far too large to be lounging around royal premises. He thinks she smells like dirt and disapproval.

"He's sticking with me," I say. "If I have to suffer, he suffers too."

Joe gives a soft woof that I choose to interpret as solidarity rather than protest.

Maggie laughs. "Poor Joe. But maybe having him there will keep Mrs. Trechón at a safe distance. Remember that growling signal."

"One hand in the air, fist closed," I demonstrate, and Joe immediately drops into his intimidation stance, teeth bared in a fearsome display. I quickly give him the release signal, and he returns to his normal, goofy self.

"I'd better go," Maggie says, checking her watch. "And you'd better not be late. Mrs. Trechón will add tardiness to her list of your duchess-ly crimes."

"The list that already includes 'inappropriate footwear' and 'excessive independence'?" I sigh. "Fine. Go investigate. Solve the case without me. I'll just be learning how to hold a teacup without disgracing the entire monarchy."

Maggie gives me a quick hug. "You'll survive. And hey, maybe you can use the time to think about motives. Why would someone want Tom dead? Who benefits most from his death? Besides Josh Thoroughgood, I mean. Keep turning it over while Mrs. Trechón makes you balance books on your head or whatever it is she has planned."

With a final wave, Maggie heads back toward the village, leaving Joe and me to face our fate. I take a deep breath and turn toward the castle.

"Come on, Joe. Let's get this over with."

Joe follows me through the grand entrance and into the magnificent foyer with its soaring ceilings and marble floors that still make me feel like an imposter every time I walk across them. How did I, Rebecca Orange, animal trainer from San Diego, end up in a literal castle with a royal title? Most days it feels like an elaborate prank that everyone but me is in on.

We navigate the maze of corridors that I'm still learning, past priceless artwork and antiques that I'm terrified of breaking. The castle staff nods respectfully as we pass, though I notice a few sympathetic glances. Word of my duchess lessons must have spread.

"You know what the worst part is, Joe?" I say quietly as we approach the Grand Ballroom. "I'm not even sure why I'm fighting this so hard. It's not like I don't want to be good at being Jack's wife. I just wish it didn't mean erasing everything that makes me... me."

Joe looks up at me with his soulful eyes, then gently bumps his massive head against my leg.

"You're right," I tell him. "We'll get through this. And then we'll get back to what we're actually good at— training animals and solving murders."

I pause outside the ornate double doors of the Grand Ballroom, straightening my shoulders and lifting my chin in what I hope is a duchess-like posture. Through the thick wood, I can already hear Mrs. Trechón's crisp footsteps pacing back and forth, no doubt rehearsing her lecture on all the ways I've failed to live up to my title in the last twenty-four hours.

"Once more unto the breach," I mutter to Joe, who sits obediently at my side, his tail giving a single supportive wag.

I push open the doors and step into the lion's den.

———

The Grand Ballroom stretches before us like an endless sea of polished marble, sunlight streaming through towering windows to illuminate every speck of dust, every imperfection— which, according to Mrs. Trechón's narrowed eyes, includes me. She stands in the center of the vast space, a rigid figure in a perfectly tailored navy suit, her spine so straight it makes my back hurt just looking at her. A pocket watch dangles from her manicured fingers, and she clicks it shut with a snap that echoes through the cavernous room.

"Three minutes and thirty-seven seconds late, Your Grace," she announces, her accent making even this simple statement sound like an indictment. "Punctuality is the courtesy of kings—and duchesses."

"I was busy working," I reply, already feeling defensive. I don't mention that the work I was doing involved solving a murder, but Mrs. Trechón seems to pick up on that fact anyway.

Her expression doesn't change, but something in her eyes hardens. "A proper duchess delegates criminal investigations to the proper authorities. She does not go gallivanting about town asking questions and drawing further attention to scandalous matters."

"Gallivanting?" I repeat, incredulous. "I would *never*," I let mock indignation flood my tone. "I prefer the term, 'scooting my caboose' around town. It has more American charm, don't you think?"

"What I think," she says, approaching me with measured steps, "is that you are avoiding your real responsibilities in favor of playing detective."

Joe, who normally backs me up in these situations with a well-timed whine or head tilt, has inexplicably settled himself in the corner of the ballroom, sitting with perfect posture, his eyes attentive but calm. The traitor.

Mrs. Trechón follows my gaze and gives a small, satisfied nod. "Your dog understands the value of proper decorum. Perhaps you could learn from him."

"Et tu, Joe?" I mutter under my breath. Then, I decide it's time to get down to business. "Fine," I say, setting my bag down by a gilded chair. "Let's get this over with. What duchess-ly skills am I deficient in today?"

"All of them," she replies without hesitation. "But we shall focus on the most pressing concerns." She glides over to a side table and picks up a stack of leather-bound books. "Your posture and gait require immediate attention. The way you entered the theater on opening night— shoulders hunched, head bobbing like a common peasant— it was remarked upon."

"By whom?" I demand, thinking about all the people sitting in the audience. *What a rude bunch of gossips!* "What kind of person has nothing better to do than critique my walking style on the same night there was a murder in the building? Don't they have enough to gossip about, what with the death of a man? Do my shoulders really take priority?"

"They do to those who matter," she says cryptically. "Now, take these."

She thrusts the stack of books into my arms. They're heavier than they look, and I stagger slightly under their weight.

"Place them atop your head," she instructs. "One at a time."

I stare at her. "You're joking. This is actually a thing? I thought book-balancing was just in movies."

"It is a time-honored method of teaching proper posture," she says, demonstrating by placing a single volume on her own perfectly coiffed head. "The spine must be straight, the shoulders back but relaxed, the chin parallel to the floor."

Reluctantly, I place one book on my head. It immediately slides off, landing on the marble floor with a loud slap. Joe's ears perk up, but he doesn't move from his spot.

"Again," Mrs. Trechón commands.

I try once more, focusing intently on keeping my head level. The book wobbles but stays in place. Small victory.

"Now walk," she says.

I take one step, then another. The book shifts precariously. Three more steps and it tumbles to the floor.

"Mon dieu," Mrs. Trechón sighs heavily. "It is like watching a newborn giraffe attempt ballet."

"As an animal trainer, I'll say that newborn giraffes are actually really graceful," I mutter, retrieving the book.

"Try again," she says. "And this time, imagine a string pulling you upward from the crown of your head. Your body should follow this imaginary line."

For the next twenty minutes, I walk back and forth across the ballroom with varying numbers of books on my head, while Mrs. Trechón offers a steady stream of corrections.

"Smaller steps."

"Do not stomp."

"Your hips should not sway like a common barmaid."

"Shoulders down."

"Not that far down!"

By the time she's satisfied with my walking, my neck muscles are screaming in protest. *I'm too old for this,* I think, wanting to throw the books at my tormentor. Meanwhile, Joe hasn't moved an inch, watching the proceedings with what looks suspiciously like amusement in his brown eyes.

"Now," Mrs. Trechón says, moving on without a moment's respite, "we shall practice entering a room and greeting dignitaries. The Malaysian Ambassador and his wife will be visiting next week, and you cannot greet them as if you are ordering coffee at a drive-through."

"When have I ever—" I begin to protest, but she cuts me off.

"The incident with the Spanish consul," she says pointedly. "You asked if he wanted cream and sugar with his tea."

"That was being hospitable!"

"That was the job of the serving staff," she corrects. "A duchess does not serve; she presides."

I roll my eyes. *I'd like to* _preside_ *you right off a cliff.*

"Let us begin," she says, positioning herself at the far end of the ballroom. "I shall be Ambassador Wong. You will enter, approach appropriately, and greet me with the correct level of formality. Begin."

I walk toward her, trying to remember everything she just taught me about posture and stride.

"No, no, no," she interrupts before I've taken five steps. "You are not strolling through a shopping mall. You are a duchess entering a room that falls silent at your arrival. Again."

I bite my lip and try once more, this time imagining myself as Katherina from *Taming of the Shrew*— but with an alternate ending where she runs away to live a life of freedom and is never heard from again.

"Better," Mrs. Trechón concedes when I reach her. "Now the greeting."

I extend my hand. "It's a pleasure to meet you, Ambassador."

Mrs. Trechón closes her eyes briefly, as if praying for patience. "Too casual. Too American. You are not welcoming him to a backyard barbecue. Again."

"I am delighted to welcome you to Monrovia, Ambassador Wong," I try, forcing a smile that feels fake even to me. "I trust your journey was comfortable?"

"Marginally improved," she says. "Though your smile resembles that of a shark considering its next meal."

"Maybe because I feel like I'm being eaten alive by these lessons," I snap.

Mrs. Trechón's eyebrows rise nearly to her hairline. "Is that how you see it? As some form of torture designed specifically to torment you?"

"Isn't it?" I challenge. "Since you arrived, all you've done is criticize everything about me— how I walk, talk, dress, breathe." I pause, thinking about the most dignified way to handle this conversation. "It just seems like this is… personal?"

A flicker of something— recognition, perhaps—crosses her face. "I am merely doing my job. You chose this life when you married the Duke."

"I chose Jack," I say firmly. "The man, not the title."

"And so you must learn to navigate society within the constraints of what you have chosen," she shrugs.

For a moment, I think about Katherina and her character's arc in *Taming of the Shrew*. She was forced to change. Is that something I'm willing to do, for Jack? Suddenly, I feel as if the wind has been knocked out of me. Is this why I haven't put more effort into planning our honeymoon? Maybe I'm not sure I can live up to the title that comes with loving my husband. Maybe, even though I walked down that aisle… I'm still… not… *sure.*

"Your Grace," Mrs. Trechón says, looking worried. "Are you feeling alright?"

No, I'm not, thanks to you, I want to say. Instead, I take a deep breath and stand as tall as I can. Then, I look her in the eyes, daring her to challenge me. "While your efforts are appreciated," I say, copying the tone I've heard Jack use when he's in a diplomatic space, "I need to find a way to be a duchess that works with who I am, not against it. I'm never going to be perfect at this— and frankly, I don't want to be. I want to be real. I am called to this title by fate, or destiny, or maybe just love. And I'm called to act the role in my own way. Not yours."

Mrs. Trechón studies me for a long moment. "Your authenticity is... not without merit," she says, as if the admission causes her physical pain. "But it must be channeled appropriately. The monarchy is not a platform for self-expression. It is an institution that has survived for centuries precisely because it adheres to certain standards."

"Standards can evolve," I suggest.

"Some can," she concedes. "Others are foundational." She gestures to the grand room around us. "This castle, this kingdom, they stand because their foundations are solid. Change too much too quickly, and the structure becomes unstable."

I hadn't expected this level of philosophical debate from Mrs. Trechón. For a moment, I see her not as my tormentor but as a guardian of something she genuinely believes in.

"So what you're saying is," I respond slowly, "You believe I should learn the rules before I choose which ones to break?"

She winces at my phrasing. "I would not have put it quite so... rebelliously. But essentially, yes. You must understand *the why* before you challenge *the what*."

It's not the validation I wanted, but it's something. A tiny bridge across the vast chasm between us.

"Lesson concluded for today," Mrs. Trechón announces, checking her watch. "We shall resume tomorrow at precisely nine o'clock."

"I have murder suspects to interview tomorrow," I say.

"Eight thirty, then," she amends, her tone making it clear this is non-negotiable. "Punctuality is—"

"The courtesy of kings," I finish for her. "And duchesses. I got it."

She gathers her materials with brisk efficiency. "Until tomorrow, Your Grace. Come prepared to discuss appropriate conversational topics for the state dinner next month. Hint: murdered actors are not among them."

With that parting shot, she glides from the ballroom, the door closing behind her with a soft but decisive click.

"Well," I say to Joe, who finally abandons his perfect posture to pad over to my side, "that was about as fun as a root canal."

Joe bumps his head against my leg sympathetically.

"And you," I tell him, scratching behind his ears, "were absolutely no help. Since when do you behave perfectly for her? You're supposed to be on my side."

He looks up at me with innocent eyes that seem to say, "I'm on your side when you have cheese to share with me."

I sigh, gathering my things. "Come on. Let's go find Maggie and get back to solving a murder. At least that's something I *know* how to do."

CHAPTER

Eight

THE NEXT MORNING, the bell above *Café de Flore's* door jingles as we push inside, the scent of cinnamon and fresh-baked pastries enveloping us. I got up early to feed the castle animals before beginning my Royal Investigator duties, and now I need caffeine more than I need oxygen. Joe trots beside me, his nose working overtime as he catalogs every delicious smell in the place. Maggie follows behind, already scanning the room for our soon-to-arrive suspect— the illustrious Brent Thoroughgood, former teen heartthrob and current murder investigation person of interest.

"If I don't get caffeine in the next five minutes, I may collapse," I announce to no one in particular.

"You always say that," Maggie replies, but she's already guiding us toward the counter where Jocelyn stands arranging a display of pumpkin-shaped cookies.

The café has transformed overnight into an autumn wonderland. Delicate orange fairy lights twinkle from the exposed wooden beams overhead, and hand-crafted wreaths adorned with dried leaves and berries hang from every available surface. Somehow, Jocelyn has managed to make fall look elegant rather than like a craft store exploded.

Jocelyn spots us and her face lights up. "My favorite investigators!" she says, her voice soft but warm. "And the most handsome dog in Monrovia, of course."

Joe's tail thumps against my leg at the recognition. He knows when he's being complimented.

"Two cinnamon lattes," Maggie orders before I can speak. "And maybe some eggs for me? I'm starving."

"Make that two eggs," I add. "Duchess lessons burn calories, apparently. Especially when they involve balancing books on your head."

Jocelyn's eyes widen. "She really made you do that? I thought that was just in movies!"

"So did I," I sigh. "And yet, here we are. My neck may never recover."

While Jocelyn prepares our drinks, she leans over the counter conspiratorially. "Maggie said when she called to reserve a table that you're meeting Brent Thoroughgood here." Her cheeks flushing conspiratorially. "Is it about the murder?"

"It is," I confirm, watching her expression carefully. "Official investigation business."

"Well, I have just the spot for you," she says, already gathering up our drinks. "Follow me."

She leads us to a secluded corner table partially hidden by a tall bookshelf stuffed with well-worn novels. It's the perfect spot for a private conversation— or an interrogation disguised as one.

"This is our most private table," Jocelyn explains, setting down our lattes. "I thought you might want some... discretion. Given who you're meeting." She blushes again, and I can practically see the teenage Jocelyn hanging posters of Brent on her bedroom wall.

"This is perfect," Maggie assures her. "Thank you."

"And for the distinguished gentleman," Jocelyn adds,

producing a massive dog cookie shaped like a bone from her apron pocket. "Fresh baked this morning."

Joe sits like the perfectly trained canine he occasionally pretends to be, waiting for my nod before gently taking the offered treat. He settles under the table, the cookie held reverently between his massive paws.

"Your eggs will be right up," Jocelyn promises, then lowers her voice again. "And I'll bring Brent right over when he arrives. Every time he comes in he's just so dreamy!"

Jocelyn scurries back to the counter, leaving us to settle in. Maggie immediately pulls out her notebook.

"So, our approach?" she asks, pen poised. "Brent only promised us fifteen minutes. Apparently he doesn't like to sit at a restaurant too long. He claims crowds of fans start to gather."

"Let's start casual," I suggest. "Get him talking about his career, his transition to serious acting. Then we can ease into questions about Josh and the understudy arrangement."

"Good cop, bad cop?" Maggie asks hopefully.

"More like 'interested fan' and 'suspicious duchess,'" I correct her. "You can gush a little if you need to get it out of your system."

"I will not gush," Maggie insists, though the slight flush on her cheeks suggests otherwise. "I am a professional."

"Says the woman who told him she loved *sand*," I remind her.

Before Maggie can defend her fan-girl moment, the bell above the door chimes again. The entire café seems to collectively hold its breath as Brent Thoroughgood makes his entrance. He's wearing designer jeans, a perfectly fitted leather jacket, and sunglasses that probably cost more than a one bedroom apartment in San Diego. Three teenage girls at a corner table immediately start whispering and pointing, not-so-subtly taking photos with their phones.

Brent ignores them with practiced ease, scanning the room

until he spots us. He weaves through the tables with the confidence of someone who knows all eyes are on him and finds it completely natural.

"Ladies," he says, his accent smooth as he slides into the chair across from us. "Thank you for suggesting somewhere local. I'm trying to 'connect with the community,' as my publicist insists– rather relentlessly, I'm afraid."

Before I can respond, Jocelyn appears at our table, practically floating. She's carrying a plate I don't recognize from the menu— some kind of fancy avocado toast with poached eggs and what looks like truffle shavings.

"Your usual, Mr. Thoroughgood," she says, setting it down with the care one might use for handling a newborn. "Just the way you like it."

Brent doesn't even look surprised. He flashes her a practiced smile that doesn't quite reach his eyes. "Being famous has its perks," he says, picking up his fork.

Maggie glances pointedly at the empty space in front of her. "I still haven't gotten my eggs," she mutters, just loud enough for me to hear.

"You might be the only person in Monrovia more famous than Joe," I observe, nodding toward my dog, who is now watching Brent's plate with undisguised interest.

Brent laughs, a sound that seems deliberately calibrated for maximum charm. "That's quite a dog. What is he, some kind of mastiff mix?"

"Tibetan Mastiff," I correct. "Pure-bred and fully aware of his own celebrity status."

"Well, he's got presence," Brent acknowledges. "Essential in this business."

"Speaking of business," I say, steering us toward the actual purpose of this meeting, "thanks for agreeing to talk with us about the production. And about Tom."

Something shifts in Brent's expression— so subtle I might have missed it if I wasn't trained to read body language in animals, which translates surprisingly well to actors.

"Terrible business, that," he says, cutting into his avocado toast. "Still can't believe it happened."

"Were you and Tom close?" Maggie asks, slipping easily into her role.

Brent shrugs. "We were colleagues. Professional. He was a decent guy. A bit eager, always asking for career advice. But respectful of my process, which I appreciated."

"Tell us about your process," I suggest. "This role is quite a departure from your action movie days, isn't it?"

Brent's posture changes instantly, straightening as he leans forward. This is clearly a topic he's prepared to discuss.

"Exactly why I took it," he says, enthusiasm creeping into his voice. "After *L'Été at Sandcastle High*, I got typecast. The pretty boy. The action hero who never gets hurt. I did those cheesy action flicks because they paid well, but there's no substance there."

"You did all your own stunts, though, right?" Maggie asks. "That must have been challenging."

"Always," Brent nods, a flash of something— pride? Pain? — crossing his face. "Never used a double. That's commitment to craft, even in a B-movie. But now I'm ready for people to see I can actually act. Petruchio is complex— he's not just a brute taming a shrew. There are layers. The kind that lead to Oscar-winning roles."

I resist the urge to roll my eyes at his pretentiousness. "And your brother? Is he also committed to the craft? It seems... convenient that he was Tom's understudy."

Brent's expression cools noticeably. "Josh has potential," he says carefully. "He just needs opportunities. That's how this business works— connections, family ties."

"Like the Wayans family, or the Franco brothers?" I suggest.

"Exactly," Brent nods, seemingly pleased I've caught his

meaning. "I admire those families. They stick together, create opportunities for each other. Why not do the same for Josh?"

"Um, apologies if this is rude to ask, but... Does Josh actually *want* to be an actor?" Maggie asks, her pen poised above her notebook.

Brent waves a dismissive hand. "If he doesn't want it now, he'll get used to it. It's a great career— when you're successful." The last part carries a weight I can't quite decipher. "Besides, it's better than what he was doing before."

"Which was?" I prompt.

"Nothing worth mentioning," Brent replies, suddenly very interested in his food. "Look, I'm not forcing him. I'm helping him. There's a difference."

Before I can press further, we're interrupted by the flash of a camera. The teenage girls have grown bolder, one of them now standing just a few feet from our table with her phone held high. A small crowd has started to form, and while it's not disruptive, Brent looks concerned. He sighs, though it seems more performative than genuine. "Hazards of the job," he says with a practiced smile. "I should probably get going before this turns into an autograph session. Don't want to distract from your important investigation."

He gestures to Jocelyn, who materializes instantly with a to-go box. The speed of the service is almost supernatural, and it tells me this show has become a regular morning routine. While Brent packs up his barely touched food, I try one last question.

"Were you with your brother the entire time before the show? When the poisoning must have happened?"

Brent's hands pause briefly in their task. "I already told the police— Josh and I were in my dressing room. Together. The whole time." His eyes meet mine, challenging. "Anything else you'd like to know?"

"Not at the moment," I say, matching his gaze. "But we may have more questions soon."

"I'm sure you will," he replies, standing smoothly. "Good luck with your investigation, Duchess. I hear that's more your element than the actual duties of your title."

The barb lands, but I keep my expression neutral. "Everyone has their talents, Mr. Thoroughgood. Mine happens to be finding the truth."

His smile tightens slightly. "Well then, I look forward to you finding it. Good day, ladies."

With that, he strides toward the door, pausing only to sign a napkin for one of the squealing teenagers. The bell jingles again as he exits, and the café seems to exhale collectively.

"Well," Maggie says, finally spotting Jocelyn approaching with our long-forgotten eggs. "That was..."

"Interesting," I finish for her, my mind already sorting through the information. "Should we see him off?"

———

We step out of *Café de Flore* into the crisp autumn air, watching as Brent Thoroughgood makes his way down the cobblestone street. Even from behind, there's something performative about his walk— each step calculated to project confidence, like he's perpetually on a red carpet. The teenage fans trail after him at a respectful distance, whispering and giggling amongst themselves. I wonder if they've heard about the murder at the theater, or if Brent's celebrity status somehow shields him from association with anything so unpleasant in their eyes.

"Well, that was informative and irritating in equal measure," I say, adjusting Joe's leash as he sniffs at a nearby lamppost with intense focus. "Did you catch how quickly he shut down when we asked about Josh?"

"Completely closed off," Maggie agrees, still frowning slightly. "And that comment about it being 'better than what he was doing before'? What do you think that meant?"

Before I can speculate, a voice calls out from across the street. "Your Grace! Ms. Lefevere!"

We turn to see Zacharia waving enthusiastically from his newsstand, his lanky frame practically folded in half as he leans over his counter. A stack of magazines threatens to topple from his precarious display.

"Should we?" Maggie asks, nodding toward him.

"Might as well," I sigh. "He always knows something useful, even if it's buried under seventeen layers of gossip."

We cross the street, Joe trotting between us with the regal bearing of a dog who just enjoyed a gourmet cookie and expects more treats to materialize at any moment. Zacharia's newsstand is, as usual, a meticulously organized chaos of publications— everything from respectable newspapers to tabloids so scandalous they'd make Mrs. Trechón faint in horror.

"I saw you with Brent Thoroughgood!" Zacharia stage-whispers as we approach, his eyes wide with excitement. "Is he a suspect? Are you investigating him for the theater murder? Did he do it? Was it for fame? Revenge? A secret love affair gone wrong?"

"Breathe, Zacharia," I advise, amused despite myself by his enthusiasm. "Yes, we're investigating. No, I can't tell you if he's a suspect."

"But you wouldn't be talking to him if he wasn't, right?" Zacharia presses, leaning even further across his counter. "I mean, you don't just have casual coffee with people during murder investigations, do you?"

"We talk to everyone involved with the production," Maggie explains diplomatically. "It's standard procedure."

Zacharia looks mildly disappointed but rallies quickly. "Well, if he is a suspect, I might have some information that could be relevant." He taps a glossy magazine half-hidden beneath more respectable publications. "The new issue of *Monrovian Whispers* just came in."

I raise an eyebrow. "The gossip magazine? Not exactly a reliable source."

"Sometimes gossip has a kernel of truth," Zacharia says defensively. "And they've got a big story on Brent Thoroughgood. Industry insiders talking about how his action movie career is completely finished."

That catches my attention. "Because he wants to do serious acting now?"

Zacharia shakes his head, lowering his voice conspiratorially. "Because he physically can't do the stunts anymore. According to their sources— and they say they've got medical records to back it up, though that seems intrusive even for them— he's got some kind of degenerative spine condition."

"What?" Maggie and I exchange a surprised look.

"It's apparently why he disappeared from films for those couple of years," Zacharia continues, clearly delighted to be delivering shocking news. "He had multiple surgeries, tried experimental treatments, everything. But it's progressive. Only going to get worse as he ages."

I process this information, thinking back to how carefully Brent had lowered himself into his chair at the café, how he'd shifted his weight with subtle discomfort when he thought no one was watching.

"The magazine says he's basically forced to reinvent himself as a 'serious actor' because action roles are physically impossible now," Zachariah adds, tapping the cover. "And eventually, even regular acting roles might be too painful if he has to stand for long periods."

"That would explain his sudden interest in theater and 'artistic integrity,'" Maggie muses.

"And why he's so desperate to get his brother into acting," I add, the pieces clicking into place. "If Brent's condition is progressive..."

"He needs someone to carry on the family name in the industry," Maggie finishes my thought. "Someone he can mentor while he still can, maybe even someone who could eventually play the roles he can't."

"Exactly!" Zacharia nods vigorously. "The magazine calls it the 'Thoroughgood Succession Plan.' Dramatic, right? But if his brother doesn't have the talent..."

"Then having him understudy a minor role in a regional production makes perfect sense," I say slowly. "It's a low-risk way to get Josh experience and credits for his resume. Unless..."

"Unless the lead understudy's role suddenly opens up," Maggie says, her eyes widening. "Because the original actor dies."

Joe whines softly at my feet, perhaps sensing the shift in our energy. I absently scratch behind his ears while my mind races.

"Can I see that magazine?" I ask Zacharia, who hands it over immediately.

The article is everything Zacharia described— anonymous sources, vague medical terminology, and dramatic predictions about Brent's career. But there's enough specific detail to make me think at least some of it is true. Especially the time-line, which shows Brent's action roles ending abruptly three years ago, followed by a two-year hiatus, and then his recent "artistic renaissance" in theater.

"Do you think Brent killed Tom to give his brother a better role?" Zachariah asks, unable to contain himself. "That would be an amazing exclusive for *The Messenger.* 'Former Teen Heartthrob Turns to Murder for Family Fame!'"

"We're not accusing anyone of anything yet," I caution, handing the magazine back. "This is all just background information."

But inside, my investigator instincts are on high alert. If Brent's condition is as serious as the article suggests, it changes everything. His insistence on getting Josh acting work isn't just nepotism— it's desperation. A man facing the end of his own career, trying to build a legacy through his less-talented brother. Would that be enough motivation for murder?

"We need to talk to Josh again," I tell Maggie quietly. "Without his brother hovering over him. And we should ask Officer Basilier to look into these medical records, see if there's any truth to them."

Maggie nods. "I'll text her now."

While she pulls out her phone, I turn back to Zacharia. "Thanks for the information. As usual, your gossip radar is impeccable."

He beams at the backhanded compliment. "Happy to help the investigation! And if you solve it, remember who gave you this lead. Page one exclusive would be nice."

"I'll keep that in mind," I promise, though we both know any official statement will go through proper channels, not Zacharia's revamped version of Rodrigo's old paper.

As we walk away from the newsstand, my mind is already mapping out next steps. If Brent has a degenerative condition that's ending his action career, it gives him a powerful motive for ensuring his brother succeeds in the industry. And if Josh wasn't naturally talented enough to earn roles on his own merits...

"You're thinking it, aren't you?" Maggie asks as we head toward the theater. "That Brent might have killed Tom to give Josh a better part?"

"I'm thinking it's suddenly a much stronger motive than simple nepotism," I reply. "A man facing the end of his career, desperate to establish his brother as his replacement? That's powerful motivation."

Joe looks up at me, his brown eyes wise and knowing. Sometimes I swear this dog understands every word we say.

Behind us, Brent's fans have long since disappeared. But somehow, I still feel like we're being watched.

CHAPTER
Nine

THE EVENING FOG rolls across the castle grounds like a gauzy theater curtain, revealing and concealing the animal menagerie in dramatic glimpses. Jack and I walk side by side, each of us carrying pails of animal feed, while Joe and Luma trot ahead, their noses working overtime to catalog the evening air. This is my favorite time of night at the castle— when the guests have gone, the staff retreats to their quarters, and the grounds belong only to us and the animals. For a brief window, I'm not the Duchess of Atwood. I'm just Rebecca Orange, animal trainer, walking with her husband and their dogs, about to feed some exotic animals. Simple. Normal. If your definition of normal includes a giraffe that only eats pasta.

"You're smiling," Jack observes, his breath creating little puffs of condensation in the cool evening air. "Should I be concerned? Last time you smiled like that, Joe had destroyed Mrs. Trechón's favorite hat."

"That was an accident and you know it," I defend, bumping his shoulder with mine. "Though I will admit, seeing her face when she found it in the garden, covered in dog slobber... that was a moment I'll treasure forever."

Jack laughs, the sound warming me more than my jacket does against the autumn chill. "You're terrible."

"And yet you married me anyway," I remind him.

"Best decision I ever made," he says, his voice dropping to a tender register. "Even if it did come with an increased likelihood of pet-related diplomatic incidents."

We reach the alpaca enclosure first, their fuzzy silhouettes materializing through the mist like something from a dream. The moment they spot us, they rush to the fence, their strange, soft humming sounds demonstrating excitement. They know food is coming. Joe and Luma sit obediently at the fence line, though Joe's tail sweeps wide arcs across the ground– he loves to see his friends.

"Ladies first," Jack says, gesturing to the wooden troughs attached to the fence.

I pour grain into the troughs, smiling as the alpacas immediately dip their heads to eat, making contented little noises that remind me of the meditation app Maggie keeps trying to get me to use. Their long eyelashes flutter as they chew, and for a moment, I'm transported back to the days when feeding time was just part of my job, not a stolen moment of normalcy in an increasingly bizarre life.

"Remember when I used to only do *this* for a living?" I ask Jack, watching as he reaches over the fence to scratch one alpaca's ears. "Take care of animals, I mean."

"Your life was simpler then," Jack agrees. "Now you're an animal trainer, *and* a Royal Investigator, *and* a Duchess. You're wearing many hats."

"And in Monrovia, the hats are big," I say. "At least my curtsy is improving. If Mrs. Trechón has her way, I'll be able to curtsy in the largest hat the land has to offer. Yesterday she compared me to a drunk giraffe trying to pick up a penny."

"Colorful," Jack says, raising an eyebrow. "And anatomically improbable. As you've told me many times, giraffes don't bend well."

"Speaking of creatures that don't bend well," I say, nodding toward the aviary just visible through the fog. "Ace is probably wondering where his dinner is."

We bid farewell to the alpacas and make our way toward the hawk enclosure. Joe and Luma follow, their noses occasionally dipping to investigate particularly interesting patches of grass. The mist swirls around our ankles as we walk, giving everything an ethereal quality that makes the castle grounds feel even more like someplace out of a fairytale— albeit one where the princess is utterly incompetent at princess-ing.

Ace spots us before we fully reach the aviary, his piercing cry slicing through the evening quiet. The red-tailed hawk sits regally on his perch, his fierce eyes tracking our approach with the precision of a living missile guidance system.

"Ready for delivery," I say as Jack opens the small container he's been carrying. Inside is a dead mouse, which he offers to me with a gallant bow. "Such romance," I deadpan, but I take the offering.

"Only the finest deceased rodents for my Duchess," he replies, grinning.

I step into the aviary— a spacious, beautifully designed structure that gives Ace plenty of room to fly while keeping him safe from predators and ensuring he doesn't decide to relocate to the village and terrify the locals. Ace watches my approach, his head tilting with that distinctive bird curiosity that always makes me smile.

"Hello, handsome," I say softly. "Dinner is served."

I place the mouse on the feeding platform, stepping back as Ace swoops down from his perch with breathtaking speed and precision. He grabs the mouse in his powerful talons and returns to his perch to enjoy his meal.

"Show-off," Jack mutters affectionately as we exit the aviary. "He always performs for you. When I feed him, he just stares at me like I'm an Uber Eats delivery person."

"That's because you're competition," I explain. "You both seek my attention. Two proud, handsome males establishing territory. Don't worry– I like you much better than Ace. His talons scratch my hand whereas your hands are very soft."

Jack snorts, shaking his head. "I'm adding that to the list of strange compliments you've given me. Right after 'you smell better than most mammals.'"

We're both laughing as we approach the giraffe enclosure, where Alfredo's head looms above the mist like a periscope from some impossible submarine. The giraffe spots us and immediately stretches his long neck in our direction, his expression somehow conveying both haughtiness and eager anticipation.

"I should never have told Chef Renauld about Alfredo's pasta obsession," Jack sighs, though his eyes are twinkling with amusement. "She's taken it as a personal challenge to create the perfect giraffe-friendly pasta dish. Did you know she ordered special semolina flour from Italy last week? Just for him and based on your suggestions?"

"I like to think my culinary challenges are keeping Chef young," I say, watching as Luma circles the picnic basket we'd left near the fence earlier.

Jack unfurls a large blanket on the grass, spreading it out beneath Alfredo's favorite viewing spot— a massive oak tree that provides the perfect height for the giraffe to peer down at us while we eat. I retrieve the picnic basket, which is surprisingly heavy, and set it in the center of the blanket.

"Chef Renauld outdid herself," Jack says as he opens the basket. "Complete Italian feast— antipasti, fresh-baked focaccia, and of course, the pièce de résistance for our interloping giraffe friend..."

He pulls out a tall, specially designed feeding bowl with an extended neck—almost like a vase— filled with perfectly cooked pasta in a light sauce. It's designed so Alfredo can dip his head and reach the pasta without having to bend uncomfortably low. "Didn't think I'd forget you, did you boy?" Jack calls up to Alfredo.

Next comes our own dinner: two covered plates of home-made ravioli that steam appealingly when Jack removes the lids, a bottle of red wine, and proper crystal glasses that seem hilariously out of place for a picnic.

"And for the furry members of our dinner party," Jack continues, producing two silver bowls containing what appears to be pasta made from zucchini and carrots, topped with small bits of chicken. "Chef Renauld insisted the dogs shouldn't feel left out."

Joe's tail thumps against the ground so hard I'm surprised it doesn't trigger seismic monitoring equipment somewhere. Even dignified Luma looks excited, her eyes following the bowls as Jack sets them down at the edge of the blanket.

"Dinner is served," Jack announces, placing Alfredo's special bowl on the raised platform next to the fence. The giraffe doesn't waste a moment, his long tongue snaking out to investigate the offering before he begins eating with surprising delicacy.

We settle on the blanket, the dogs happily munching at their special pasta while Jack pours wine into the crystal glasses. The fog has lifted slightly, revealing a sky scattered with stars just beginning to appear. In the distance, the castle's windows glow with warm light, and somewhere an owl hoots softly. It's perfect— so perfect it almost makes me forget about murdered actors and backstabbing theater companies and the crushing weight of duchess expectations.

Almost.

"So," Jack says after we've both had a few bites of ravioli, which is somehow still perfectly warm despite our outdoor setting. "How's the investigation going? Any leads on who might have poisoned your actor?"

I sigh, setting down my fork. "I've got an update on our main suspect, Brent Thoroughgood. Turns out Mr. Perfect

Hair has a degenerative spinal condition that's ending his action movie career. According to gossip— which we still need to verify— he's transitioning to 'serious acting' because he physically can't do stunts anymore."

"And you think that gives him even *more* motivation to kill, beyond just wanting his brother to have the part?" Jack asks, refilling our wine glasses. "Still seems extreme for such a small role."

"Yes, but this new information means Brent might have been desperate," I think out loud. "Desperation does strange things to people. If Brent's facing the end of his career and his brother isn't talented enough to succeed on his own merits..."

"You need to find proof," Jack says, his expression serious now. "Speculation won't be enough, especially with someone as high-profile as Brent Thoroughgood."

"I know," I sigh. "Officer Basilier is looking into his medical records and the timeline of his career changes. She's still waiting on the toxicology report to verify the poison was added to the cup and wasn't already present in the wine bottle. Maggie and I are planning to interview Josh alone tomorrow, to see if we can get him to talk without his brother hovering."

Jack nods, then seems to hesitate before asking his next question. "And... are you regretful at all we've postponed our honeymoon?" He offers a small smile, framing the question casually. "I know many a lady has regretted missing out on time with yours truly. I wouldn't want you to withhold any feelings of missing out..."

"Of course I'm sad about it," I say, trying to put into words what I've only recently come to realize. "It's just..."

"What?" Jack's eyes are hopeful. He's sensed something off in me. Now, he might get the answers he's been seeking.

"It's–" I stumble, choosing my words carefully. "*You're* perfect," I motion at him. "*We're* wonderful together. I'm so *thrilled* to be married to you. I just– I guess I don't want to fail.

I didn't expect that the word Duchess would come with such a weight. I suppose I was only thinking about my own happiness, being with the person I love–"

"I did warn you," Jack adds, his eyes somber. "I warned you about what this would entail."

"Of course you did!" I exclaim. "But I never really *understood* what you'd gone through until people starting looking at me like, like–"

"Like you are lucky to be in a role they can't imagine?" Jack nods, deep understanding crossing his face. "And even though it should make you want to impress them, to live up to their every expectation, it only makes you…"

"… makes you want to rebel!" I say, finishing the sentence for him. "It makes me want to do something wild. Something they'd never expect. It makes me want to be ferociously myself! To insist on being me without apology. Jack," I lean in, shaking my head. "I think I'm going crazy. I've never felt so full of anarchist spirit. How is that being Royal can make me want to light everything on fire?"

Jack laughs. "Now you know why I drowned my feelings with booze and women on a yacht for years. I *did* warn you," he says again.

"I think I've been putting off the honeymoon because it's what they'd expect," I say, shrugging. "And solving this murder means–"

"It means you're still *you*," Jack sighs, running a hand through his hair. "Well, I'm relieved to learn it's not that you don't want to be around me. I was beginning to think I smelled."

"I work around wild animals," I smirk at him. "You couldn't possibly smell worse than the alpacas." I pause, my thoughts circling something important. "It's not you. It's that solving this murder shows I can't be tamed. I don't want to end up like Katherina, from *Taming of the Shrew*. Does that make sense?"

Jack straightens his posture, raising one eyebrow in that way of his I can never resist. "As a man who has spent his life in a cage, it most certainly does. And, Rebecca, we *can* do this our own way. My Aunt is quite agreeable. We could get rid of Mrs. Trechón and hire a press secretary to shift the public image in whatever way you like! I wish you'd let me call the Queen–"

"No," I say, waving a hand in the air. "That's you coming to my rescue. I need to save *myself* from being the wrong kind of Duchess."

Jack's about to open his mouth, and I can almost *hear* the coming protest when–

A figure approaches in the distance. A figure that immediately makes me lose my appetite.

"Your Grace!" a voice cuts through our moment like a blade through butter. "*Qu'est-ce que c'est?* What is this?"

Mrs. Trechón strides across the lawn, her perfect posture making her look like she's floating rather than walking. She emerges from the fog like my personal nightmare. Even in the dim evening light, I can see the horror on her face as she takes in our picnic setup.

"We're having dinner, Mrs. Trechón," Jack answers before I can speak, his voice carrying the polite authority he reserves for situations when he's annoyed but can't show it. "With Alfredo. Because we want to. And– as the Duke and Duchess– we're in charge here. Not. You."

Mrs. Trechón's gaze travels from us to the giraffe, who is happily slurping pasta from his special bowl, completely unconcerned with human drama. "Duchesses do not dine outdoors," she states, as if reciting from some ancient royal rulebook. "Especially not on the ground. With animals."

"I believe this Duchess does," I reply, gesturing to the evidence all around us.

"It is unseemly," Mrs. Trechón continues, her nostrils flaring slightly. "What if someone were to see? What would they think of the monarchy?"

"That we enjoy feeding our animals and spending time together?" Jack suggests, his tone light but with an undercurrent of steel.

"That the Duke and Duchess of Atwood have no respect for tradition or propriety," Mrs. Trechón corrects. "The evening meal is a formal affair. There are protocols, standards—"

Jack looks at me, trying to gauge my reaction.

"I've got this," I tell him, adding in a whisper. "I don't want the Queen to hate me before our one year anniversary."

Jack seems as if he wants to say more, but then he sighs and begins gathering our plates, muttering under his breath, "Not even a picnic without an audience." I help Jack finish packing. Together, we begin to walk away, hand-in-hand, the dogs at our feet. But I pause before we make our way back to the castle. "Wait here," I say to Jack. Then, I turn back toward Mrs. Trechón, who's still standing on the grass, her arms crossed.

"Your Grace?" she asks. "Anything I can do to accommodate your dining this evening? Perhaps I could have the staff set the table."

"The only thing you can do," I say to her, leaning in, "is tread more carefully. You may have a direct line to the Queen... but I know where to find hungry lions."

"Your *Grace?!*" she says, horrified. "Duchesses... do not... make threats."

"Neither do ladies-in-waiting, but you seem to have forgotten that," I say. "So it seems the Queen would be quite unhappy with both of us. In which case, I say we call it even."

With that, I turn on my heel, sliding my hand back into Jack's– where it belongs.

CHAPTER

Ten

THE NEXT DAY arrives with the subtle cruelty of a hangover, though I haven't had a drop to drink. Last night, the interrupted picnic with Jack left me feeling I might have gained the upper-hand with Mrs. Trechón, but this morning's scheduled lesson with her has proven otherwise. Instead of arriving cow-towed and shameful– as I hoped she would– she showed up to our lesson with a two-hour, very-pointed lecture on "The Proper Dining Habits of Duchesses Throughout History." It seems standing up to her has only made her worse.

Sitting through her presentation has left me with a dull headache and a fierce determination to solve this murder case if only to prove that my "unseemly interests" have value. Joe seems equally tired, his massive head hanging slightly lower than usual as we stand outside the Royal Theatre, waiting for Maggie to arrive with the caffeine that might save this day from complete disaster.

"You look like you've been trampled by a herd of your alpacas," Maggie announces cheerfully as she approaches. Somehow, she looks fresh and put-together. *Probably because she didn't have to spend two hours training with Mrs. Trechón this morning.* Her blonde braids are perfect, her outfit is coordinated, and her smile is offensively bright.

"That would have been preferable to Mrs. Trechón's lecture," I grumble. "Did you know that in 1837, the Duchess of Mirabelle caused a national scandal by eating an apple outdoors? Apparently, she was nearly stripped of her title. I'm warned the same could happen to me!"

"How scandalous," Maggie says, handing me a steaming paper cup that smells divine. "Well, here's something to cheer you up. Coffee from *Café de Flore* and a croissant from Henri at *Le Petit Scone.*"

I accept both with the reverence of a pilgrim receiving holy relics. "Henri, another one of my biggest fans."

"No, you've won him over," Maggie shrugs, unwrapping her own croissant. "He actually sent his well-wishes. Though he did mention that Joe's tail knocked over an entire tray of eclairs last time you visited."

I glance down at Joe, who manages to look simultaneously innocent and vaguely guilty. "That was months ago. And I paid for every eclair."

I take a bite of the croissant, and despite my determination to remain grumpy, I have to admit it's perfect— crisp exterior giving way to a buttery, flaky interior that practically melts on my tongue. Henri may be a grouchy traditionalist who thinks I'm corrupting Monrovian culture with my American ways, but the man knows his pastry.

"So," Maggie says, checking her watch, "Officer Basilier called this morning. The toxicology reports came back on the wine."

"And?" I ask, immediately alert despite my fatigue.

"Definitely poisoned. Some kind of fast-acting neurotoxin mixed into the cup itself, not the bottle. It was specifically targeted at Tom."

"Which confirms our theory that someone with access to the prop table or the stage did this," I say, my mind already clicking through possibilities. "What about Brent's medical records?"

Maggie looks around cautiously before lowering her voice. "Officer Basilier couldn't officially access those, but she has a contact at the insurance company that handles film production policies. They said Brent was dropped from their coverage three years ago due to a pre-existing condition. Seems to corroborate Zacharia's story."

"So the gossip magazine was right," I muse.

"Exactly. And get this— before coming to Monrovia for this production, Brent was rejected for five different film roles because he couldn't get insurance. This theater gig might be his last chance at career redemption."

I take a thoughtful sip of coffee. "And if his brother becomes successful in theater, Brent could leverage that connection to stay relevant, maybe even get directing roles or producing credits."

"A family legacy," Maggie agrees. "When his own body betrays him too much to perform anymore."

The picture is becoming clearer, but something still doesn't feel right. Would Brent really poison someone just to get his brother a minor role?

"Before we talk to Josh, let's start with Cosmo," I say decisively. "He's at the center of everything that happens in that theater, and he might have overhead some gossip he hasn't seen fit to share."

"Hence our early morning theater visit," Maggie agrees. "Jenny mentioned he'd be here testing lighting cues from 7 a.m."

We finish our breakfast and approach the theater's stage door. Unlike yesterday, when the building hummed with activity, today the entrance is quiet, almost eerily so. The door is unlocked, which seems strangely trusting given recent events, but I guess murder doesn't change all routines.

"Hello?" I call out as we step inside, Joe padding silently

beside me. The backstage area is dimly lit, most of the work lights off, creating pools of shadow that make the already maze-like corridors more disorienting. "Cosmo?"

No answer greets us, but I can hear the faint hum of electronics somewhere in the building.

"Maybe he's on stage?" Maggie suggests, leading the way through the dark hallway. "Or in the booth?"

We step into the wings of the stage, which is illuminated by a single ghost light— the solitary bulb theaters traditionally leave on when the stage is otherwise dark. It casts long shadows across the set pieces, making the temporarily deconstructed Petruchio's house look like something from a horror film rather than a Shakespearean comedy.

"This is creepy," I whisper, though I'm not sure why I'm whispering. "Cosmo knew we were coming, right? Why wouldn't he turn on more lights?"

Joe's ears perk up suddenly, his massive head tilting as he focuses on something I can't hear. Then I catch it, too— voices, raised in what sounds like an argument, coming from somewhere above us.

"The lighting booth," Maggie mouths, pointing toward the back of the theater.

We move quietly through the wings and out into the house— the audience section— where the argument becomes clearer. Two voices bounce off the theater's acoustically designed walls, neither person aware of how well sound carries in this space. One is unmistakably Jenny's, her usual theatrical brightness sharpened into something harder and more desperate. The other is Cosmo's, sounding more assertive than I've heard him before.

Rather than announcing our presence, I catch Maggie's eye and place a finger to my lips. She nods, understanding immediately. Sometimes the best investigative technique is simply to listen. We creep up the aisle toward the back of the theater, where a door leads to the technical booths over-looking the stage.

"—my ONE CHANCE, Cosmo!" Jenny's voice rings out as we approach. "Do you understand that? Twenty-five years I've been waiting for this opportunity! Twenty-five years of community theater in church basements and high school auditoriums, and finally, FINALLY, I have a real budget, a real theater, and royal patronage!"

"I understand," Cosmo responds, his voice weary but firm. "I've *been* there for all twenty-five of those years, Jenny. Don't question my commitment to you! I'm doing everything humanly possible. I'm the lighting designer, the PR company, the costume department, the props master, the stage manager—"

"And you're wonderful at all of it," Jenny cuts in, her tone switching abruptly from anger to something saccharine and gentle. "That's why I *need* you. You're the only one who truly understands..."

There's a quiet moment in which nothing is said. The silence makes me wish I could see them. But as quickly as it happened, the moment passes.

"You know how I feel," Cosmo says, his voice almost a whisper. "There's nothing more I can do to prove it to you. I've given you my all. Not just through the costumes. The lighting. The cleaning. I've scrubbed this theatre top to bottom. And then, of course, there's the thing I can't say–"

"We are NOT discussing that now," Jenny hisses, cutting him off sharply. "Not here."

There's a pause, heavy with something I can't quite identify.

"You promised me this would be the ticket," Cosmo says, his voice dropping so low we can barely hear him. "You asked, and I delivered. I've given you my very *soul*."

"I know," Jenny says, her voice somber. "That's why we can't give up yet. We have to make this work. Too much has already been sacrificed. We're *this* close!" She exclaims, and I imagine her holding up her fingers an inch apart. "*This* close to everything I've ever wanted!"

The conversation feels like we're only getting half the story, references to something neither of them will name directly. *What secrets are Jenny and Cosmo keeping?*

My thoughts are interrupted by Joe, who has apparently decided that eavesdropping is boring. He lets out a massive yawn that ends in a small, involuntary whine. It's barely audible to me, but in the theater's perfect acoustics, it might as well be a foghorn.

The voices above us go silent immediately.

"Hello?" Jenny calls out sharply. "Is someone there?"

No point in hiding now. "Good morning!" I call back, trying to sound casual, like we've just arrived. "It's Rebecca and Maggie. We had an appointment with Cosmo?"

Footsteps approach the booth window, and then Jenny's face appears, peering down at us. In the dim lighting, her expression is difficult to read, but her body language radiates tension.

"Your Grace!" she exclaims, her voice instantly transforming into her usual enthusiastic lilt. "What a delightful surprise! I didn't realize you were coming by so early."

She disappears from the window, and moments later, the door at the top of the stairs swings open. Jenny emerges, wearing a pleated skirt covered in tiny avocados paired with bright yellow legwarmers. Her smile is dazzling, showing not a hint of the anger we overheard seconds ago.

"We have a very busy day ahead," she chatters as she descends the stairs toward us. "Costume fittings this morning, then a complete run-through this afternoon. Everyone's working so hard to keep the momentum going— such dedication in the face of adversity! It's truly inspiring."

She reaches us, still beaming that too-bright smile. Up close, I can see the slight smudges of her mascara, the tension lines around her mouth that her cheerful facade can't quite hide. She's exhausted and desperate. A dangerous combination.

"I hope you've had a chance to consider allowing our little production to continue?" she asks, her eyes fixed on mine. "In Tom's memory, of course. A tribute to his talent."

"I haven't made a decision on the play's future yet. We're still gathering information about the murder," I say diplomatically. "That's why we've come to speak with Cosmo."

"Of course, of course," Jenny nods vigorously. "Cosmo's absolutely indispensable to our production. I don't know what I'd do without him!" She laughs, the sound slightly brittle. "He knows every detail of how this theater runs. If anyone can answer your questions, it's him!"

She glances at her watch with exaggerated surprise. "Oh my! Look at the time. I have a meeting with our press office in twenty minutes. I'd better dash!"

Without waiting for a response, she squeezes my arm, nods at Maggie, and hurries toward the exit, her skirt swishing around her knees as she practically flees the theater. The door slams behind her with surprising force, leaving an awkward silence in her wake.

"That was... interesting," Maggie says once Jenny is safely gone.

"Very," I agree, looking up toward the booth where Cosmo still hasn't appeared. "Shall we?"

We climb the stairs to the lighting booth, where we find Cosmo hunched over a complex-looking control panel, pretending to be deeply absorbed in his work. His mustache looks particularly droopy this morning, and the bags under his eyes have bags of their own.

"Good morning," I say, intentionally gentle. "I hope we're not interrupting anything important."

Cosmo straightens up slowly, like a man whose spine protests every movement. "Your Grace. Ms. Lefevere." He nods to each of us in turn. "Nothing that can't wait. Jenny has me running lighting tests for some special effects she's added to the final scene."

"Added recently?" Maggie asks, her notebook already in hand.

Cosmo sighs heavily. "It's part of Jenny's process, God bless her." Despite his annoyance, there's a fondness in Cosmo's eyes when he mentions Jenny. "Everything changes constantly. New blocking, new lighting cues, new costume elements. It's always been Jenny's way, but with the pressure of this production..." He trails off, rubbing his eyes tiredly.

"We were hoping to ask you a few questions," I say. "About Tom, and about the night of the poisoning."

Cosmo glances around the cramped booth, which is filled with equipment, cables, and what appears to be a half-eaten sandwich. "Would you prefer to go somewhere more comfortable? The green room, perhaps?"

"Actually," Maggie interjects, "we'd prefer somewhere private. Some of our questions are... sensitive."

Cosmo's shoulders slump slightly, as if he'd expected this but had been hoping to avoid it. "The lighting booth is the most private place in the theater," he says, gesturing around the small space. "No one comes up here but me."

"Perfect," I say, stepping fully into the booth with Joe at my heels. The space immediately feels cramped with my enormous dog added to the mix, but Joe simply curls himself into a compact ball in the corner, watching us with concerned eyes. Joe may be laying down, but I can tell by his alert ears that he's on guard.

Cosmo closes the door behind us with a soft click, the sound somehow ominous in the confined space. With the door shut, the booth feels like a confessional—small, private, and designed for revealing secrets.

"So," he says, settling heavily into his chair. "What would you like to know?"

CHAPTER
Eleven

THE LIGHTING BOOTH door clicks shut behind us, sealing us into the small space. I suddenly realize how claustrophobic the lighting booth is, and I feel sorry for whoever spends the entire show up here. Cosmo settles into his chair, the vinyl squeaking under his weight as though protesting the added pressure. Even in the dim light, I can see the exhaustion etched into every line of his face. *Poor Cosmo needs a vacation*, I think.

Maggie perches on the edge of a stool, notebook ready, while I lean against the console, careful not to accidentally flip any switches that might plunge the theater into darkness— or worse, trigger whatever special effects Jenny has planned for the final scene.

"So," I begin, keeping my tone conversational, "did Tom have any enemies that you know of? Anyone who might have had a grudge against him?"

Cosmo blinks slowly, like the question takes effort to process. "Tom? No, not at all. He was the ideal cast member, really. Always on time, knew his lines, respected the props."

"No arguments with other cast members? No tension with Brent or Josh Thoroughgood?" Maggie presses.

"Nothing serious." Cosmo shrugs, his shoulders barely moving, as if even this small gesture costs him energy he can't spare. "There was the usual theatrical ego stuff— Brent wanting more spotlight, Tom occasionally suggesting line readings— but nothing that would..." His voice trails off, unwilling to finish the thought.

"Nothing that would lead to murder," I finish for him.

"Exactly." He nods, his mustache bobbing with the movement. "It was all just typical theater politics. Nothing personal."

"What about the cup?" Maggie asks, her pen hovering above her notebook. "Officer Basilier mentioned it was left unattended twice— once on the prop table and again on stage. Did you notice anyone hanging around either location who shouldn't have been there?"

Cosmo's brow furrows, creating deep canyons in his forehead. "I wish I could say yes. That would make this all easier, wouldn't it? But no, I was running around like a madman that night." His hands gesture vaguely, encompassing the countless tasks he was juggling. "Lighting cues, costume repairs, prop placement— I barely had time to breathe, let alone monitor who was near the prop table."

"You're doing a lot of jobs," I observe. "Why not hire more staff?"

A bitter laugh escapes him. "Budget. Always budget. Jenny stretched every penny to get this production off the ground. Most of the crew is either volunteers or working for far less than they're worth." He glances down at his hands, which I notice are covered in small cuts and calluses. "I don't mind, though. This is Jenny's big chance. I'm happy to help however I can."

There's something in his voice when he says Jenny's name — a softening, almost reverent. I've heard that tone before, usually from lovestruck teenagers or particularly devoted golden retrievers. It's the sound of complete, unwavering loyalty.

"You've worked with Jenny for a long time," I say. It's more statement than question.

"Twenty-five years," he confirms, a sad smile lifting one corner of his mouth. "I was her lighting designer on her very first production— a disastrous version of *Our Town* in a church basement with lights we borrowed from a hardware store." The memory seems to briefly energize him. "The fire marshal nearly shut us down, but Jenny talked him into giving us one more chance. She's always been... persuasive." A smile plays at the corner of his mouth.

"Twenty-five years is a long time to stay with one director," Maggie comments casually, though I can tell she's probing.

"Jenny is special," Cosmo says simply. "She sees things in people that others miss. When my marriage fell apart and my drinking got... problematic, no one else would hire me. Jenny gave me a second chance when I didn't deserve one. I'll never forget that."

I exchange a quick glance with Maggie. This feels important— not just Cosmo's devotion to Jenny, but the suggestion that his past might make him vulnerable.

"That's admirable," I say. "Her loyalty to you."

"And mine to her," he adds quickly, a slight defensive edge creeping into his voice. "Which is why I agreed to this interview, even though..." He hesitates, then seems to come to a decision. "Even though I wasn't thrilled about being questioned like a suspect." There's a defensive edge to his voice.

"We're questioning everyone involved with the production," Maggie assures him.

"I understand," Cosmo nods. "And I appreciate your thoroughness. But I also wanted a chance to remind you how much this production means to all of us." He leans forward slightly, his eyes suddenly more alert. "Your Grace, I know this is an awful situation. A tragedy. But letting the show continue would mean *everything* to Jenny. She's waited her entire career for this moment."

"I understand that," I say carefully. "But a man is dead."

"And we *all* mourn Tom," Cosmo says quickly. "But canceling the show won't bring him back. It will only punish everyone else who's worked so hard. Think of the cast and crew!"

Joe shifts in his corner, perhaps sensing my growing discomfort with the conversation's turn.

"The press has been calling, you know," Cosmo continues, his tone casual but his eyes watchful. "Asking questions about the new Duchess and her support for the arts in Monrovia. Whether your patronage was just a formality or a genuine commitment."

I feel the subtle pressure in his words, the implied threat that my decision could affect my public image. Mrs. Trechón would probably have a coronary if she heard a prop master attempting to manipulate a duchess, but I have to admire Cosmo's strategy. He knows exactly which buttons to push.

"I, of course, haven't responded to those inquiries yet," he adds softly, leaning back and crossing his arms. "I thought it best to wait until we had clarity on the situation."

"That was thoughtful of you," I reply, keeping my expression neutral. "I'm sure the palace PR team appreciates your discretion."

Joe raises his massive head, his eyes fixed on Cosmo with sudden intensity. He doesn't growl, but there's a stillness to him that I recognize— he's sensing something in Cosmo's body language that he doesn't like. Joe's always been an excellent judge of character, especially when someone's not being entirely forthcoming.

"Well," I say, standing straighter and deliberately breaking the tension, "Thank you for your time, Cosmo. You've been very helpful."

"Have I?" he asks, sounding genuinely curious.

"Sometimes what people don't say is just as informative as what they do," Maggie replies with a smile that doesn't quite reach her eyes.

Cosmo looks between us, clearly trying to decipher that cryptic response, before finally nodding. "Well, I'm happy to help any way I can. For Jenny's sake. And for the production."

"We can find our way out," I tell him, already moving toward the door, eager to escape the booth's stifling atmosphere. "Good luck with those lighting cues."

Joe unfolds himself from his corner, stretching briefly before padding to my side. As we exit, I notice he keeps his massive body between me and Cosmo, a subtle protective gesture that speaks volumes.

The door closes behind us, and I let out a heavy exhale.

The staircase creaks under our feet as we descend from the lighting booth, each step seeming to voice its own opinion about our investigation. Maggie walks ahead, her blonde braids swinging with relief as we put Cosmo behind us. Joe brings up the rear, his nails clicking softly against the wooden steps. The theater feels different now— more secretive, as if the building itself is keeping confidence with whoever poisoned Tom Prink.

"Well," Maggie says once we're far enough from the booth, "Cosmo certainly has a thing for Jenny, doesn't he? Twenty-five years of devotion. That's either true love or Stockholm syndrome."

"Maybe both," I mutter, still processing the subtle pressure tactics Cosmo employed. "Did you notice how he casually threw in that bit about the press asking questions? As if I didn't have enough people trying to shape my public image."

"Speaking of which..." Maggie slows her pace, turning to face me on the landing. "We do need to make a decision about the show. Are you going to allow it to continue?"

I sigh, running a hand through my hair. "Honestly, I don't know. Every option feels wrong somehow."

"It's complicated," Maggie acknowledges. "Politically speaking, shutting down the production could be seen as you withdrawing support from the arts. Which, given your nascent duchess reputation—"

"The papers are calling me the 'Duchess of Death.' I'm not sure allowing a production where someone was murdered to continue is going to improve matters."

We reach the bottom of the stairs, pausing in the shadowed corridor that leads back toward the stage. The theater is eerily quiet, with only the distant hum of the air conditioning system to remind us the building is alive. Joe's ears are perked, swiveling like satellite dishes as he monitors sounds I can't hear.

"Maybe we'll solve the murder and *then* you can restart the show," Maggie thinks out loud. "We're close."

I close my eyes briefly. "Something still feels off about this whole situation. I can't put my finger on it, but we're missing something."

Joe's sudden bark interrupts my thought, a sharp sound that echoes down the corridor. His head is turned toward a branching hallway, body alert but not tense.

"What is it, buddy?" I whisper, moving to his side.

Then I hear it— a voice muttering, frustrated and low. We exchange glances before quietly moving toward the sound, Joe leading the way with the stealth that always surprises people given his massive size.

We round the corner to find Josh Thoroughgood pacing a small section of hallway, script in hand, lips moving as he struggles through his lines. He looks nothing like the polished, confident actor his brother pretends to be. His shirt is rumpled, hair sticking up at odd angles where he's clearly been running his hands through it in frustration, and his face is pinched with concentration bordering on panic.

"What s-seekest thou?" he reads, stumbling over the archaic language. "Or what would'st thou? I—no, thy name?" He shakes his head, flipping back a page. "That's not right. What seekest thou? Or what would'st thou? Thy name? No, that's not it either!"

He scratches his head violently, like he's trying to physically dislodge the correct words from his brain. Joe watches this display with his head tilted to one side, the canine equivalent of puzzled concern.

"What seek—would'st—thy name?" Josh tries again, voice cracking. "Why don't they just say, 'who are you' like normal people?"

The frustration in his voice is painfully genuine. I almost feel like we should offer to help, but this is also a perfect opportunity to observe him unaware. Either he's a phenomenal actor playing the part of an incompetent one, or he genuinely isn't prepared for this opportunity. *So much for talent running in the family,* I think.

Josh consults the script again, mouthing words silently before attempting out loud: "What seek... no, what seekest thou, or what would'st... would'st thou have? Or what's thy name?"

He pumps his fist in quiet triumph at finally getting the line right, only to immediately deflate as he moves to the next section. "Request? The meaning of his... no, this..." He groans, slapping the script against his thigh.

After another moment of struggle, he glances at his watch and mutters something that sounds like a curse. With a defeated sigh, he tucks the script under his arm and slips through a nearby door that must lead to one of the dressing rooms.

"Well," Maggie whispers once he's gone, "that was painful. I think I need a drink after watching that."

"He's really not ready for this role," I agree. "Doesn't look like someone who'd commit murder for a part he can't even handle."

"Or," Maggie suggests, "he's realizing he's in over his head *after* the fact. Maybe he or Brent thought this would be his big break, but now that he's got the role..."

"He's panicking," I finish. "Either way, I think we should talk to him. Without his brother hovering nearby. Josh clearly lacks Brent's polish and media training. He might just tell us the truth if we approach him the right way."

Joe woofs softly, as if adding his vote of approval to this plan.

"Good call, Joe," I say, scratching him behind his ears. "Let's go see what the less famous, more anxious Thoroughgood has to say for himself."

We move toward the dressing room door, and I feel a small surge of anticipation. Sometimes the quietest people have the most revealing stories to tell.

CHAPTER

Twelve

I TAKE a deep breath before knocking on Josh Thoroughgood's dressing room door, still processing the pitiful scene we just witnessed in the hallway. The man clearly has no business being in a Shakespeare production— or any production that requires memorizing words more complex than "Would you like fries with that?" Joe stands beside me, his massive head tilted slightly as if he, too, is wondering what kind of suspect struggles this much with iambic pentameter.

My knuckles rap against the wood, and there's a startled "Just a minute!" from inside, followed by the sound of something— possibly several somethings—falling to the floor. When the door finally cracks open, Josh Thoroughgood's face appears in the gap, flushed and glistening with sweat. His eyes widen when he sees us.

"Oh! Your Grace! And, um, Ms. Lefevere." He clutches his script to his chest like a shield, using it to fan himself frantically. "I didn't realize... I mean, I wasn't expecting... is there something I can help you with?"

"We'd like to ask you a few questions," I say, keeping my

voice gentle. The man already looks like he might bolt at any sudden movement. "Do you have a moment?"

His eyes dart from me to Maggie, then drop to Joe, who's watching him with unblinking intensity. "Is the dog... friendly?" Josh asks, his voice rising an octave.

"Only to people who haven't committed murder," Maggie says cheerfully. I shoot her a look, and she mouths "What?" with exaggerated innocence.

"Joe is perfectly friendly," I assure Josh, giving my dog the training signal for 'belly flop.' Joe immediately softens his gaze and lets his tongue loll out in what I call his "harmless goofball" expression, then rolls over on his back and kicks his legs into the air. "He just likes to meet new people."

Josh hesitates, then opens the door wider. "Come in, I guess. Sorry about the... everything."

The dressing room is surprisingly barren for someone who's been cast in a production for weeks. There's an ancient-looking couch with stuffing escaping from multiple tears, a wobbly makeup table with a single script and water bottle on it, and a rack holding exactly three items of clothing— all of them costumes, not personal items. No photos, no knickknacks, no coffee mug with a witty theater quote. Nothing that says "Josh Thoroughgood works here."

Joe immediately makes a beeline for the couch, circling once before settling his enormous bulk onto the cushions. There's an ominous creaking sound, and Joe's eyes go wide with alarm as the couch sinks dramatically beneath him. He freezes, looking at me as if to say, "Do I get up, or will that make it worse?"

"It's fine," Josh says, noticing Joe's distress. "That's been broken since before I got here. It won't collapse completely. Probably."

Joe gives me a skeptical look but settles in, his massive head resting on the arm of the couch like he's posing for a portrait titled "Mastiff on Couch."

"You haven't really moved in, have you?" Maggie observes, gesturing to the stark room.

Josh laughs, a nervous sound that escapes like air from a punctured tire. "No. I... I never thought I'd be here this long, to be honest. I was sure I'd get fired day one."

"Well aren't you an optimist," I laugh, leaning against the makeup table, which feels sturdier than it looks.

"Everyone knows I'm terrible," he says with such immediate candor that I'm momentarily taken aback. "I'm a terrible actor. I can't remember lines— you probably heard me out there, struggling with basic sentences. I can't hit my mark. I have no idea what I'm doing half the time." He runs a hand through his disheveled hair, and for a moment, I see traces of his brother in his face. Then, the echoes of Brent disappear, and Josh hunches over again. "I can't even tell a convincing lie, let alone pretend to be a whole different person for two hours straight."

I exchange a quick glance with Maggie. This level of honesty from a murder suspect is refreshing, if somewhat confusing.

"Then why did you agree to be in the show?" Maggie asks, settling into the room's only chair.

Josh's eyes dart away from us, suddenly finding the floor fascinating. "Brent thought it would be a good idea," he says, his voice dropping in volume. "He actually wanted me to have a bigger part initially, but I talked him down to understudy for a minor role. I figured I could just... hang around. Watch. Learn. I never expected to actually perform!"

"But now you have to, because Tom is dead," I say, watching his reaction carefully.

Josh pales visibly, swallowing hard. "Yes. And I'm going to ruin everything. I keep telling Jenny I can't do it, but she won't listen. Says I'll 'find my way into the character,' whatever that means. Right now I can barely find my way down the hallway!"

"A friend of ours works for one of the gossip magazines," Maggie says casually, though I can tell by the slight tilt of her head that she's watching Josh intently. "He mentioned there's a rumor going around that your brother has some kind of condition. Something that might prevent him from continuing his action movie career."

The effect on Josh is immediate and dramatic. His eyes go wide, the script slips from his fingers and falls to the floor, and his mouth opens and closes several times before any sound emerges.

"You know?" he finally whispers, looking like he might collapse. "How does anyone know? We've been so careful..."

"So it's true?" I press gently.

Josh's face crumples, tears welling in his eyes. "I shouldn't say," he chokes out.

"Josh," I lean in, using my most convincing voice. "If you don't tell us, we're going to find out anyway. I'm in the papers all the time, and trust me– they never fail to release a story like this."

"It's awful," he breaks down, sinking onto the edge of the couch beside Joe, who shifts slightly to make room. "Brent's been in pain for years, hiding it from everyone. The doctors say it's only going to get worse. No more stunts, no more action roles. Eventually, he might not be able to stand long enough to act at all."

Joe lifts his head, looking at Josh with what I swear is genuine concern. He can hear the pain in Josh's voice. I'm always amazed that animals sometimes have more empathy than humans.

"And that's why he wanted you to start acting?" I ask.

Josh nods miserably, wiping his nose with the back of his hand. "Everyone in our family depends on Brent's income. Our parents, our sister and her kids. When he got sick, he started thinking about the future. Thought maybe if he could establish me in the industry, I could... I don't know, take over somehow." He laughs bitterly. "As if I could ever fill his shoes."

"What did you do before this?" Maggie asks.

"I scooped ice cream at a Creamery in the Cotswolds," Josh says with a sigh. "And I was good at it. Customers liked my waffle cones. But I can't support a family on that."

"So your brother pushed for you to be cast here," I say, trying to piece together the timeline. "As Tom's understudy."

"He said he thought this experience might make me fall in love with acting." Josh looks up suddenly, his eyes frantic. "Wait a second. You don't think I... that I would..." He shakes his head violently. "I didn't kill Tom! Why would I? This is the worst thing that could have happened to me! Now I actually have to perform, and I'm going to humiliate myself, my brother, and probably destroy his last chance at a legitimate comeback!"

His distress feels genuine. Either Josh Thoroughgood is a much better actor than he claims, or he truly didn't want Tom's role.

"Your Grace," he says, suddenly leaning forward, his voice dropping to a desperate whisper. "Please don't let the show continue. Just shut it down. Tell everyone it's out of respect for Tom or because of safety concerns or whatever you want. Just don't make me go out there." His eyes dart toward the door before he adds, "Please. Before someone else gets hurt."

I feel my pulse quicken at those words. "Someone else? Do you think Tom's death wasn't an isolated incident?"

Josh's face goes slack, as if he's suddenly realized he's said too much. "I just meant... I'll probably hurt myself tripping over the set or something." He looks at me again, desperation in his expression. "This play is dangerous. It's cursed. You can't let it keep going."

"Josh," Maggie says, her voice gentle but firm, "if you know something about Tom's death—or if you're worried about another person being in danger— you need to tell us."

He shakes his head, suddenly looking exhausted. "I don't know anything. I just... I have a bad feeling. This show isn't meant to go on." He trails off, his gaze unfocused. "Nothing good can come from continuing it."

The room falls silent except for Joe's gentle snoring—apparently, he's decided the interrogation is boring enough to warrant a nap. I study Josh's face, trying to read beneath his obvious anxiety. He might be hiding something. But is it knowledge of who killed Tom, or something else entirely?

———

We leave Josh's dressing room in silence, the weight of his strange confession hanging between us. Joe gives a massive shake, as if trying to dislodge the tension that had built up in that tiny room, his collar jingling like distant wind chimes. I wait until we're well out of earshot, navigating the narrow backstage corridor, before finally turning to Maggie with raised eyebrows. "Well, that was... illuminating? Confusing? I'm not sure what adjective best describes a suspect who admits he's terrible at the job he supposedly murdered someone to get."

"Contradictory," Maggie suggests, her notebook already open as she jots down observations while walking. "Either he's the world's worst actor playing the world's best role as the world's worst actor, which is *very* Shakespearean, or..."

"Or he genuinely didn't want Tom's part," I finish, ducking beneath a low-hanging set piece that looks like a partially constructed balcony. The backstage area is eerily quiet now, most of the crew apparently at lunch or working elsewhere. Our footsteps echo on the worn wooden floors, occasionally accompanied by the distant sound of hammering from some unseen corner of the building.

"Did you catch that thing he said at the end?" Maggie asks. "'Before someone else gets hurt.' That's not exactly the phrasing I'd expect from someone worried about tripping over props."

"I noticed that too." I pause, letting Joe sniff at a rack of elaborate Renaissance costumes. He seems particularly interested in a velvet doublet. He sniffs it, then rubs his back against the costume rack like a bear trying to scratch an itch on a tree. "Down, Joe. Mrs. Trechón would be ashamed. You're a duchess's dog now."

Joe reluctantly moves away from the tempting velvet, but keeps glancing back at it as if calculating whether the scolding would be worth the satisfaction.

"I don't think Josh killed Tom," I say, resuming our path toward the exit. "The level of anxiety we just witnessed isn't something you can fake. He's genuinely terrified of going on stage."

"Unless that's exactly what he *wants* us to think," Maggie counters. "Maybe he's not worried about acting— maybe he's worried about getting caught if the play continues and attention stays on the production."

We emerge from the warren of backstage corridors onto the main stage, the ghost light still casting long shadows across the set. The theater feels impossibly large and empty from this vantage point, the rows of vacant seats stretching out before us like a silent, judgment-passing audience.

"Or," Maggie says slowly, her pace slowing as an idea forms, "Maybe Josh is trying to protect Brent somehow." Maggie taps her pen against her notebook. "Think about it— Josh said his brother is getting worse. What if performing in this production is actually dangerous for Brent? What if it could accelerate his condition?"

"So Josh poisons Tom, creating a scandal that he hopes will shut down the show before his brother can injure himself further," I muse, the pieces clicking into a possible pattern. "But instead, Jenny insists on continuing, and now Josh is stuck in exactly the position he was trying to avoid."

"It would explain why he seemed genuinely upset about Tom's death while simultaneously begging you to cancel everything," Maggie points out.

"And that cryptic warning about someone else getting hurt," I add. "He could be worried about his brother."

Joe suddenly stiffens beside me, his ears perking up as he stares intently into the wings. A moment later, I hear it too— a soft shuffling sound, like someone trying very hard to move quietly. I place a finger to my lips, signaling Maggie to stay silent. Whoever's lurking backstage might have just heard our entire murder theory.

"We should continue this outside," I say at normal volume, deliberately casual. "I could use some fresh air."

Maggie catches on immediately. "Good idea. It's getting stuffy in here."

We make our way down the steps at the front of the stage and up the center aisle, Joe keeping pace between us. I can feel his body language shift to protective mode, his head swiveling occasionally to glance back at the stage. Someone is definitely watching us leave.

"Do you think Brent knows?" Maggie asks quietly as we push through the lobby doors into the bright afternoon sunshine. The contrast between the theater's dim interior and the clear day outside is jarring, like emerging from a cave.

"Knows what? That his brother might have killed someone to protect him?" I shake my head. "I can't imagine Josh would confess something like that."

Joe sniffs the air, his attention caught by something across the street. I follow his gaze to see a familiar figure disappearing around a corner— Cosmo, moving with surprising speed for a man who looked exhausted earlier.

"Was he following us?" I wonder aloud.

"Or just running around doing one of his many jobs?" Maggie suggests.

"This case keeps getting more complicated," I sigh, running a hand through my hair.

"Just another day in the life of the Duchess of Death," Maggie quips.

Joe nudges my hand with his nose, a gentle reminder that he's here, ready to help. At least one member of my investigation team never doubts himself.

"Let's head back to the castle," I decide. "I need to update Jack and figure out what to do about this production. If Josh is right and someone else is in danger, I can't in good conscience let the show go on."

As we walk away from the theater, I can't shake the feeling that we're missing something obvious— something hiding in plain sight, just like whoever was lurking in the wings, listening to our every word.

CHAPTER
Thirteen

THE CASTLE LOOMS against the darkening sky as Maggie, Joe, and I trudge up the winding path toward the service entrance. My brain feels like an overworked muscle, sore from trying to piece together contradictory evidence and cryptic warnings. After a day of interrogations and theories that lead nowhere, all I want is a hot meal, a glass of wine, and five blessed minutes without someone calling me "Your Grace" or reminding me which fork to use for which course. Even Joe looks exhausted, his usual prancing trot reduced to a plodding walk, his golden fur dulled by the fading light. Murder investigations are apparently hard on everyone, dogs included.

"I checked the Duke's calendar while we were walking," Maggie says, swiping through her tablet as we reach the rear entrance. "He's still tied up with that French trade representative. The meeting was supposed to end an hour ago, but you know how these diplomatic types are."

"Let me guess— they're still exchanging elaborate compliments while pretending not to notice the time?" I sigh, holding the door open for Joe, who gives me a grateful look as he squeezes his bulk through.

"Exactly that," Maggie confirms. "The notes say they're discussing agricultural imports, but I guarantee they're mostly talking about wine and cheese while avoiding any actual decisions."

My stomach growls loudly enough that both Maggie and Joe turn to look at me. "Sorry," I mumble. "I just realized we never actually ate lunch."

"You haven't visited the staff dining hall in awhile," Maggie suggests, a conspiratorial gleam in her eye. "Chef Renauld mentioned she's making her famous beef bourguignon tonight."

The thought of Chef Renauld's beef bourguignon— tender chunks of meat that fall apart at the mere suggestion of a fork, swimming in a sauce so rich it should have its own tax bracket— makes my mouth water instantly. It also sounds infinitely more appealing than eating alone in my royal quarters while Mrs. Trechón hovers nearby, critiquing my posture.

"Absolutely," I agree. "But let's grab Luma first. If Jack's still in meetings, she's probably going stir-crazy in their quarters."

Maggie nods, and we take a quick detour to the Duke's private wing. Sure enough, when we peek in, Luma is sitting by the door with the patient resignation of a dog who knows she's been forgotten for something "important." The moment she spots Joe, her entire body wags with joy, her collie elegance temporarily abandoned in favor of pure canine excitement.

"Poor girl," I coo, kneeling to scratch behind her ears. "Did the important Duke leave you all alone to talk about boring trade agreements? Me too!"

Luma responds by trying to lick my face off, which I take as confirmation.

"Come on," I tell her, clipping a leash to her collar. "We're going to get dinner with the *cool* people."

The staff dining hall occupies a corner of the staff building past the gardens. It's a spacious room with high ceilings and enormous windows that frame the moon rising over the hedges. Unlike the castle's formal dining rooms used for state functions, with their imposing portraits and rigid table arrangements, the staff hall feels lived-in and comfortable. Long wooden tables invite communal dining, while the stone walls are hung with a charming mishmash of photographs documenting castle events through the years— holiday parties, staff picnics, the occasional royal photobomb. It's exactly the kind of place where you can laugh too loudly without fear of diplomatic incident.

Several staff members look up as we enter, their expressions ranging from surprise to delight. Douglas, the head groundskeeper, waves us over to a table where he's sitting.

"The Duchess has arranged a visit?! And she's not in her formal wear? I'm disappointed, eh?" Douglas says, starting to rise, but I wave him back down.

"Please, no standing or bowing or 'Your Grace'-ing," I plead. "I'm just Rebecca tonight, okay? A very hungry Rebecca who's heard rumors of beef bourguignon."

The staff exchange glances but quickly relax, making room for us at their table. Joe and Luma settle beneath, their tails thumping against the stone floor in perfect harmony.

"You've got good timing," Monique, head of cleaning, tells me. "Chef just brought out a fresh batch."

As if summoned by the mention of her culinary creation, Chef Renauld emerges from the kitchen, her eyes widening slightly at the sight of us before her professional demeanor reasserts itself.

"Rebecca" she smirks at the sight of me. "Got tired of the folded napkins in the Duke's dining hall, I suppose?"

"I still can't figure out which fork to use," I tell her honestly.

"Well don't worry," Chef Renauld winks at me. "There is always enough in my kitchen, and here you only get one fork.

I'll bring you something wonderful. And perhaps a treat for your four-legged companions as well."

She disappears back into the kitchen, returning moments later with two steaming bowls of the promised bourguignon, accompanied by fresh bread still warm from the oven. The aroma alone is enough to make my eyes roll back in happiness.

"And for the distinguished canines," she adds, setting down two smaller bowls containing what appears to be the same bourguignon, though I notice she's removed the garlic and onions. "Meat only, with a touch of the sauce. No harmful ingredients."

Joe practically levitates with excitement, while Luma offers a polite tail wag that doesn't quite hide her eagerness.

"You've made their day," I tell Chef Renauld. "Possibly their entire year."

She gives a satisfied nod. "Dogs appreciate good cooking. Unlike some human food critics I could name."

I lift my fork, poised to take my first heavenly bite, when a voice cuts through the dining hall's comfortable hum.

"What exactly do you think you're doing?"

The voice has the effect of a bucket of ice water. Mrs. Trechón stands at the entrance to the dining hall, her ramrod-straight posture somehow making her seem taller than she is. Her eyes are fixed on me with laser-like intensity, her mouth a thin, disapproving line.

The entire room falls silent. Even Joe and Luma pause in their enthusiastic eating, sensing the sudden tension.

"Having dinner with my *friends*," I reply, trying to keep my voice light. "Would you care to join us? Chef Renauld's bourguignon is amazing."

"A duchess does not dine in the *staff* hall," Mrs. Trechón says, each word precisely enunciated as if she's speaking to a particularly slow child. "It is completely inappropriate. You have private dining quarters for a reason."

"I don't want to eat alone," I counter, feeling heat rise to my cheeks. "Jack is in meetings, and I'd rather have company."

"That is not my concern," she says dismissively. "What is my concern is maintaining the proper order and dignity of this household. There are centuries of tradition—"

"Oh good, another lecture on centuries of tradition," I mutter, just loudly enough for Maggie to hear. She suppresses a smile, quickly taking a sip of water to hide it.

"—that clearly need to be reinforced," Mrs. Trechón continues as if I hadn't spoken. "Which is why I've taken the liberty of doubling your etiquette lessons for the coming week. We clearly have significant work to do."

My fork clatters to the plate. "What was that?"

"Doubled your lessons," she repeats, a hint of satisfaction creeping into her voice. "Beginning tomorrow, eight a.m. sharp. We will focus on appropriate dining protocols and the importance of maintaining proper boundaries between yourself and the staff."

She gives Maggie a pointed look, as if to suggest my friendship with her is part of the problem.

"Now, if you'll excuse me, I have matters to attend to." With that parting shot, she turns on her heel and marches out of the dining hall, her footsteps echoing on the stone floor like tiny hammers nailing my coffin shut.

The silence that follows her exit is awkward enough that I want to crawl under the table and hide with the dogs.

"Well," Douglas finally says, "I believe that's what the gardening staff calls getting pruned."

The entire room bursts into laughter. Someone throws a bread roll at me from across the table, and for the first time in a long time, I feel like myself again. *I needed this*, I think. The Castle staff aren't just friends. They're family.

"I hate to say it," Maggie says, leaning close, "but your

bourguignon is getting cold, and that might be the greater tragedy here."

I pick up my fork again, though my appetite has significantly diminished at the idea of extra lessons with Mrs. Trechón. Joe nudges my leg with his nose, his bowl already licked clean, his eyes full of canine concern.

"You know," Maggie says thoughtfully, her voice low enough that only I can hear, "I was checking the staff calendar earlier today, and unless it's changed, Mrs. Trechón is supposed to be attending the Duchess of Harrington's charity auction this evening. It's across town at the Monrovian Art Museum."

I glance at her. "What are you saying?"

"I'm saying," Maggie replies, a mischievous gleam in her eye, "that we're pretty good at investigating murder suspects. Maybe we should use those skills to figure out why Mrs. Trechón has such a vendetta against you."

As her words sink in, an idea begins to form— a reckless, possibly terrible idea that would horrify Mrs. Trechón even more than my dining choices.

"Maggie," I say slowly, "I think it's time we did some reconnaissance on the enemy territory."

Joe looks up at me, as if to say he's already on board with whatever scheme I'm hatching. Even Luma seems interested, her intelligent eyes moving between Maggie and me. Maggie's idea is a great one. Such a great one that it's made my appetite return.

"We'll snoop after dinner," I add, finally taking a bite of the now-cooling bourguignon. "Even investigators need to eat before breaking and entering."

———

The staff wing of the castle exists in a strange middle ground — nicer than any apartment I could have afforded in San

Diego, but distinctly less opulent than the Royal quarters. The hallway stretches before us like the corridor of a high-end hotel, all tasteful sconces and muted colors, the carpet thick enough to muffle our footsteps as Maggie leads our little investigative team toward Mrs. Trechón's apartment. Joe and Luma pad silently beside us, apparently sensing the need for stealth without being told. It's moments like these when I wonder if the dogs understand more English than they let on.

"How do you know which one is hers?" I whisper, eyeing the identical doors that line the corridor.

"Head of household," Maggie reminds me, tapping her chest. "I know where everyone sleeps. I have to, in case of emergencies." She pauses outside a door marked 417. "This is it. Mrs. Trechón's villain cave."

"Are we sure she's not in there?" I glance nervously up and down the hallway, suddenly aware of how difficult it would be to explain why the Duchess of Atwood is loitering outside her etiquette instructor's door.

"The charity auction doesn't end until 11 p.m., and it's only 9:15 p.m.," Maggie assures me, checking her watch. "Plus, I texted Monique from housekeeping to confirm Mrs. Trechón left in the castle car thirty minutes ago."

"Okay," I nod, turning to Joe. "You're on guard duty, buddy."

Joe sits at attention, his ears perked forward, his eyes alert. I kneel in front of him, holding his massive head between my hands to ensure I have his full attention.

"If you smell Mrs. Trechón coming— or anyone else— I need you to growl. Not your scary growl," I clarify quickly. "Just your warning growl. You know the difference."

Joe gives a soft woof that I choose to interpret as understanding. For good measure, I add, "And if she somehow gets past you, bark once, loudly."

He nudges my hand with his wet nose, a gesture that seems to say, "I've got this covered. Go commit your crime."

"Good boy," I whisper, giving him one last scratch behind the ears. "We won't be long."

Maggie produces a key card from her pocket, catching my raised eyebrow. "Master access," she explains. "For emergencies."

"Is snooping on the Duchess-police an emergency?" I ask.

"I'd call it necessary reconnaissance," Maggie replies with a grin, sliding the card through the reader. The lock clicks softly, and the door swings open just enough for us to slip inside, Luma following closely on our heels.

My first impression of Mrs. Trechón's apartment is that it's exactly what I expected, yet somehow still disappointing. The living room is immaculate in a way that feels sterile rather than clean. Everything is in shades of grey and taupe, from the precisely arranged throw pillows on the sofa to the bland landscape paintings hanging at mathematically perfect intervals on the walls. There are no personal photos, no books left open, no coffee cup abandoned on a side table. If personality were color, this room would be beige.

"It's like a hotel room," I whisper, running a finger along a completely dust-free shelf. "Or a furniture showroom. Does she actually live here, or just pose in it occasionally?"

"Let's check the kitchen," Maggie suggests, moving toward the adjoining room.

The kitchen is equally impeccable— spotless countertops, not a dish in the sink, appliances that look like they've never been used. The refrigerator contains neatly labeled containers of food, arranged by expiration date, and a single bottle of expensive white wine. Even the fruit in the bowl on the counter looks like it was selected for aesthetic value rather than taste.

"This is... sad," I murmur, taking in the perfect, empty space. "It's like she's playing house, but doesn't know how people actually live."

"Look at this," Maggie calls softly from where she's examining a small desk in the corner. She holds up a leather-bound planner. "She still keeps a paper schedule. Everything color-coded and written in perfect penmanship."

I peer over her shoulder at the planner, where each day is meticulously divided into time blocks labeled with activities like "Correspondence (30 min)" and "Review of Royal Protocols: Chapter 7 (45 min)." There's even a block labeled "Personal Reflection (15 min)" that somehow manages to make self-reflection sound like a chore to be completed rather than a natural process.

"I feel like I'm getting a clearer picture of why she's so..." I search for a diplomatic word and fail. "...intense."

Luma, who has been sniffing around the apartment with the methodical attention of a crime scene investigator, suddenly perks up. Her nose twitches, and she pads purposefully toward a closed door on the far side of the living room. She scratches at it once, then looks back at us expectantly.

"The bedroom?" I guess, moving toward the door. "What is it, girl? Did you find something?"

I push the door open just a crack, and Luma immediately sticks her nose through the gap, nudging it wider. The bedroom continues the theme of sterile perfection— a precisely made bed with hospital corners, matching nightstands with nothing on them but identical lamps, a dresser with not so much as a stray earring atop it.

But Luma isn't interested in any of that. She trots directly to the far wall, which is partially hidden by the open door. As I push the door wider, I gasp.

"Oh my God," I breathe. "Maggie, come look at this."

The wall behind the door holds the one thing completely out of place in Mrs. Trechón's perfect, controlled environment: a vision board. But not just any vision board— a shrine to royalty. Magazine cutouts of tiaras, castles, and royal families are meticulously arranged on a large cork board. Headlines proclaim "Inside the Royal Life" and "Secrets of Palace

Etiquette." There are fabric swatches that look like they came from royal ceremonial attire, paint chips in regal purples and golds, and— most surprisingly— several photos of Mrs. Trechón herself, carefully photoshopped into royal settings.

"This is... very creepy," Maggie whispers, standing beside me. "It's like a teenage girl's fantasy board, but created with the precision of a serial killer."

"Look at this one," I point to a faded magazine clipping framed on the wall beside the board. Unlike the other items, this one isn't a fantasy— it's an actual article from what appears to be a society magazine dated twenty years ago. The yellowed headline reads: "ROYAL HEARTBREAK: PRINCE PHILLIP ENDS ENGAGEMENT TO LADY'S COMPANION."

The photo shows a much younger Mrs. Trechón, smiling with rare warmth, her arm linked with a handsome man wearing a formal uniform adorned with medals. They look happy, in love— nothing like the rigid, joyless woman who lectures me about proper fork placement.

"Prince Phillip of Luxembourg," Maggie reads, squinting at the caption. "Broke off engagement to Élisabeth Trechón after a six-month whirlwind romance. Sources say the Prince's family did not approve of the match, as Trechón was merely a lady's companion to the Duchess of Harrington, and, although she had noble blood, was not from a Royal family."

"The Duchess of Harrington," I repeat. "The same one whose charity auction she's at tonight?"

"Seems she's still in touch with her," Maggie confirms, her voice soft with realization. "She puts herself around royalty wherever she can. Weird, isn't it?"

The pieces click into place with sudden clarity. Mrs. Trechón was once on the verge of becoming what I am *now*— a woman who married into royalty. But she lost her chance, her dream. And now she has to watch me, someone she clearly considers unsuitable, living the life she wanted.

"No wonder she hates me," I murmur. "I'm everything she wanted to be, but I don't even want it the way she does."

"And you got the prince," Maggie adds. "Or at least, the duke."

From the hallway comes a sound that freezes my blood— a low, rumbling growl. Joe's warning signal.

"Someone's coming," I hiss, backing away from the vision board. "We need to go. Now."

We scramble to leave everything exactly as we found it, Maggie carefully closing the bedroom door to its original position while I usher Luma toward the exit. The front door opens with agonizing slowness, and we slip out into the hallway where Joe is standing alert, his eyes fixed on the corridor's end.

"Good boy," I whisper, giving him a quick pat as Maggie pulls the door shut behind us. "Let's move."

We hurry down the hall in the opposite direction, turning the corner just as we hear the distinct sound of heels clicking on the hard floor of the main corridor. The four of us press ourselves against the wall around the corner, hardly daring to breathe as the footsteps approach Mrs. Trechón's door.

There's a pause, then the sound of a key card sliding, followed by Mrs. Trechón's voice muttering something in French that sounds irritated. Through the gap between wall and corner, I catch a glimpse of her frowning at her door, then pushing it open with a suspicious glance around the hallway.

"The door was unlocked," Maggie mouths to me, her eyes wide.

My heart hammers in my chest as we wait for the inevitable shout of discovery, but it never comes. Instead, Mrs. Trechón's door closes with a soft click, and silence falls over the corridor once more.

"That," I exhale shakily, "was too close."

Joe nuzzles my hand, as if to say, "I did my job, didn't I?"

while Luma simply looks pleased with herself for her investigative prowess.

"We should get out of here," Maggie suggests, still whispering despite the fact Mrs. Trechón is out of earshot.

"I know," I agree. "But I can't lie… it felt good to be all up in her business for once. The tables have turned, am I right?"

Maggie blinks at me, clearly not understanding the phrase "the tables have turned." She misses most of my American idioms.

"Tables?" she says, worried. "Should we have turned them while we were in there?"

"Come on," I laugh, grabbing her elbow and pulling her down the corridor. "I'll explain it to you over a croissant."

A GENTLE MORNING rain pings against *Café de Flore's* windows. I'm thankful to be inside. We beat the morning crowds and grabbed the best table next to a warm fire crackling in the corner, nestled between bookshelves. I'm on my second lavender latte and still feeling the effects of last night's Mrs. Trechón espionage mission. Although I feel triumphant that we discovered her secret, I'm also... ashamed and a little horrified.

Joe sprawls under the table, occasionally sighing with the profound boredom of a dog who'd rather be chasing squirrels than solving murders. *I can relate, buddy.* I'd rather be doing almost anything than waiting for Officer Basilier to arrive and tell us we have zero usable leads in this increasingly bizarre case.

"You're stress-drinking that coffee," Maggie observes, not looking up from her tablet. "That's your tell. When you're nervous, you drink whatever's in front of you like it's water."

"First of all, rude," I reply, setting down my cup with exaggerated care. "Second of all, entirely accurate. I'm still thinking about Mrs. Trechón and those magazine clippings. It gave major serial killer vibes, didn't it?"

"Yes," Maggie says, her voice dropping to a whisper as she leans across the table. "Mrs. Trechón makes so much more sense now. She's a jilted almost-royal with a vision board of the life she never got to have. It's no wonder she's obsessed with you."

"I feel bad for her," I admit, absentmindedly tearing a croissant into increasingly tiny pieces. "Watching someone else live your dream must be torture. Especially when that someone is *me*— the walking embodiment of 'how not to duchess.'"

"Speaking of which," Maggie glances at her watch, "did you tell Jack about our little breaking-and-entering adventure?"

"Absolutely not," I say, horrified at the thought. "He'll want Mrs. Trechón fired immediately. And I need some time to figure out–"

"What?"

"What to do," I shrug. "On the one hand, her vision board is totally creepy. On the other hand, to get her fired I have to admit to the Queen I broke into her apartment, which isn't exactly duchess behavior. And clearly the royal life means so much to Mrs. Trechón. If she loses this job, it might push her over the edge! I don't want to be the person who ruins her life."

"But right now she's ruining *your* life," Maggie rolls her eyes. "Her lessons are literal torture. And I wouldn't be surprised if she has a duchess outfit with your measurements already hanging in her closet, just waiting for you to have a convenient 'accident.'"

The idea sends a chill down my spine.

"Don't even joke about that," I shudder.

Maggie shrugs. "I'm just saying… be careful."

Joe suddenly lifts his head from his paws, his ears perking forward like furry satellite dishes. A moment later, the café door swings open, and Officer Basilier strides in with her usual purposeful gait. She's wearing her uniform today, the dark blue fabric pressed to military precision, her utility belt equipped with what seems like enough gear to survive a zombie apocalypse. Several café patrons glance up nervously as she passes, perhaps mentally reviewing their recent parking violations.

"Orange. Lefevere." She nods at each of us in turn as she pulls out a chair. Her eyes drop to Joe under the table. "Dog."

Joe responds with a gentle woof of acknowledgment. They have a mutual respect thing going on.

"Coffee?" I offer, already signaling to Jocelyn behind the counter.

"Black. No sugar," Officer Basilier replies, then adds with the barest hint of a smile, "Please."

That 'please' represents significant character development in our relationship. The first time we worked together, Officer Basilier considered me a murder suspect and royal imposter. Now I've definitely grown on her. *We're practically besties.* The thought makes me smile.

"Orange, why are you smiling like a loon?" Officer Basilier asks, immediately popping my bubble.

"Just thinking about how far we've come," I say honestly.

"Well, stop it," Officer Basilier responds. "You're creeping me out."

Jocelyn delivers Officer Basilier's coffee with impressive speed, along with a fresh plate of pastries that nobody ordered but everyone appreciates.

"So," I say, once Jocelyn is out of earshot, "please tell me you have something useful on the toxicology? Because our interviews have only made the case more complicated."

Officer Basilier sets a folder on the table between us, flipping it open to reveal a collection of photographs and lab reports. "Got the lab results on the murder weapon," she says, tapping a particularly scientific-looking document with several highlighted sections. "The poison in Tom's cup was a heavy metal cleaner typically used in industrial settings. Extremely toxic. Just one sip would be enough to kill."

"Industrial cleaner?" Maggie frowns, leaning forward to examine the report. "That's not something you'd find in your average household cleaning cabinet."

"Exactly," Officer Basilier nods. "It's specialized. Used for cleaning metalwork, removing corrosion from machinery. Not the kind of thing most people have access to."

"But a theater might," I suggest, the pieces clicking into place. "For cleaning metal set pieces, props, lighting equipment?"

"Bingo," Officer Basilier says, taking a long sip of her coffee. "And here's the interesting part— the poison was only found in the cup, not in the wine bottle. Which means—"

"Whoever poisoned Tom did it backstage, before the show started," I finish her thought. "They doctored his specific cup backstage, not the wine before the show."

"So it was definitely targeted," Maggie adds. "Not a random act or a case of someone trying to poison multiple people. It had to have been someone who had access to the cup backstage in the time it was left unattended."

Officer Basilier nods grimly. "It seems our initial suspect list was a good one. This was personal. Someone connected with that play wanted Tom Prink dead, specifically."

Joe shifts beneath the table, his large paw coming to rest on my foot as if offering silent support. He's sensitive that way, always knowing when a conversation has taken a darker turn.

"We have a theory about that," I say, glancing at Maggie. "Or rather, two competing theories involving the Thorough-good brothers."

"The teen heartthrob and his less photogenic sidekick?" Officer Basilier raises an eyebrow. "I'm listening."

Maggie and I take turns explaining our suspicions— how Brent might have killed Tom to give his brother a better role and bring publicity to the show, while Josh might have done it to sabotage the production entirely and protect his brother from worsening his condition.

"It's like a sibling murder-off," I conclude. "Each with a motive that makes sense."

"Hmm," Officer Basilier says, her expression unreadable as she digests our theories. "The publicity angle is interesting. Especially considering recent developments."

"What developments?" I ask, instantly alert. My stomach churns.

"You haven't seen?" Officer Basilier says, her mouth dropping open. "Honestly Orange, you're the play's patron. I'd have thought you'd at least set up a Google alert–"

"Hey!" Maggie says, offended. "We've been a little busy investigating a murder over here."

"Seen *what?*" I say, my palms suddenly sweaty.

"The play's gone viral," Officer Basilier says, nodding toward Maggie's tablet. "Look up 'Restart the Shrew' online."

Maggie's fingers fly across her tablet screen. Her eyebrows shoot up toward her hairline. "Oh wow," she breathes, turning the screen so I can see.

A professional-looking website fills the display, dominated by a dramatic black-and-white photo of the theater with a single spotlight illuminating the empty stage. Bold text proclaims: "RESTART THE SHREW: A Movement to Save Art in Monrovia." Below that, a counter shows over two thousand signatures on a petition addressed to *me*— or rather, to "Her Grace, the Duchess of Atwood"—begging for the production to continue.

"They're trying to pressure me into letting the play go on?" I say, scrolling through the slickly designed pages. "What, like I'm some kind of monster because I want to solve the murder of an innocent man before letting the play continue? This is *worse* than being called the Duchess of Death."

"Keep scrolling," Officer Basilier instructs. "The video testimonials are particularly moving."

Maggie taps on a video thumbnail, and suddenly Brent Thoroughgood's perfectly chiseled face fills the screen. He looks appropriately somber, his eyes glistening with what I'm sure he believes are convincingly genuine tears.

"The arts have always been a beacon in dark times," he intones with practiced emotion. "Tom would have wanted the show to go on. He was a true artist, a professional to the end. By continuing this production, we honor his memory and refuse to let darkness win." His voice catches on the last word, and he looks away from the camera, presumably overcome. Then, he turns his beautiful face back to the screen his eyes boring through the lens. "I'm speaking directly to the Duchess of Atwood, now. Your Grace. It's time to restart the play. Let. Art. *Win.*"

My heart pounds in my chest. "How dare he call me out like this in public! We just *saw* him at this very café. He could have said something then!"

"It's alright, Your *Grace*," Officer Basilier smirks. "Everyone at this table knows you're not a monster attacking the arts. You have many flaws, and I'm happy to list them–"

"-- please don't–"

"But attacking the arts isn't one of them."

We click through several more videos— cast members, crew, even random citizens of Monrovia who probably couldn't pick Tom out of a lineup but are nonetheless devastated by the "attack on our cultural heritage from our own Duchess."

"Wait, go back," I say suddenly as a familiar face flashes past. "Is that Monica?"

Maggie navigates back to the previous thumbnail, and sure enough, Monica Blanchart's delicate features appear on screen. Unlike her energetic, commanding stage presence as

Katherina, in this video she appears small and vulnerable, her voice barely above a whisper.

"Tom was... kind," she says, her dark eyes swimming with tears that track silently down her pale cheeks. "He always helped me when I struggled with my lines. He believed in this production when others doubted. I need to finish this play for him. Please, Your Grace." She looks directly into the camera, and I feel an uncomfortable pang in my chest. "Please let us honor Tom's memory by sharing his final theatrical passion with the world."

A single tear makes its way down her cheek with such perfect timing that I'd be impressed if I weren't so suspicious.

"Wow, she's good," Officer Basilier comments. "Is she *always* that convincing?"

"She was just as good when we interviewed her," I say, shaking my head. "Again, she could have mentioned restarting the play *then* if she was so concerned! I want to know who's behind this," I continue, suddenly angry. "They're acting like it's my fault the play is on pause, when the truth is, there's a murderer on the loose! I can't just let the play continue when someone involved likely killed Tom! I'd be sending a murderer up on stage. And what kind of Duchess would *that* make me?"

"The Duchess of Death?" Maggie offers helpfully.

"You two should explore this," Officer Basilier thinks out loud. "Whoever started this campaign wants the play to go forward, and... why? Is it to cover up evidence?"

Maggie continues exploring the website, clicking through to the contact information. "Look who owns the domain!" she says, horror in her voice. "JennyJayProductions. Our ambitious director strikes again."

"I knew she was mad at me, but I didn't think she'd take it this far," I say, impressed despite myself. "Murder happens, production shuts down, website launches, publicity machine activated. It's almost like—"

"Someone planned it," Officer Basilier finishes my thought, her eyes narrowing. "Makes you wonder, doesn't it? I'll have the Police Department dig deeper into the digital forensics. We might be able to get more information on Jenny's company and the website she started. We'll check their financials. Maybe we can subpoena her IP address and search history."

"We'll go back to the theatre today," Maggie agrees. "Interview the suspects again."

"And confront everyone about this website!" I add, still fuming.

"If you need backup, let me know," Officer Basilier says. "I could always rough someone up a little. Good cop, bad cop, terrifying dog." She nods toward Joe, who chooses this moment to yawn widely, displaying his impressive array of teeth. Officer Basilier leans in, her hands making a little tower in front of her face as she thinks.

"What?" I ask, knowing an idea forming when I see one.

"I was just thinking," Officer Basilier adds, "maybe you *should* restart the play."

"You want me to continue a production where someone was murdered?" I stare at her incredulously. "That seems like the opposite of what law enforcement would typically advise."

"Think about it," Officer Basilier says, her voice dropping lower. "Whoever killed Tom did it for a reason connected to that play. Whether it was to give Josh a better role, generate publicity, or sabotage the production— the motive is tied to the performance."

"So if we restart the show..." Maggie begins, her eyes widening with understanding.

"We might flush out the killer," I finish. "Use a new opening night as bait."

"Exactly." Officer Basilier nods approvingly. "Announce that the show will go on, that you're supporting the arts in

Tom's memory. See who gets nervous, who gets excited, who suddenly develops an interest in industrial cleaning products."

I chew my lip, considering the strategy. It's risky— potentially putting other cast members in danger. But it also makes a certain kind of sense. If the killer's motive is tied to the play itself, then removing the play removes their motivation to act again. But reinstating it might push them to make a mistake.

"What if someone else gets hurt?" I ask. "I'd be responsible."

"Not if we're watching," Officer Basilier says firmly. "We'd have multiple officers on site, undercover. You'd have your massive fur alarm system." She nods toward Joe, who thumps his tail appreciatively against the floor. "And we'd know what to look for this time."

The idea settles in my mind, taking shape. It's exactly the kind of plan Mrs. Trechón would hate— the Duchess of Atwood deliberately putting herself adjacent to a murder investigation rather than sipping tea at a safe distance. But it's also exactly the kind of plan that might work.

"You know what?" I say finally. "I think I'll give the people what they want. The Duchess of Atwood is about to become a passionate advocate for continuing theatrical traditions in the face of tragedy."

"Mrs. Trechón will be thrilled," Maggie says with a knowing smirk.

"Mrs. Trechón can add it to her list of my duchess-crimes," I reply, thinking of that sad, meticulous vision board hidden behind her bedroom door. "Right after 'eating with the staff' and 'investigating murders instead of practicing curtsies.'"

Officer Basilier gathers her files, sliding them back into her folder with military precision. "I'll start making arrangements for security at the theater."

"Roger that, Officer," I say with a mock salute that earns me an eye roll.

As Officer Basilier stands to leave, she hesitates, then says in an unusually gentle tone, "Be careful, Orange. Whoever killed Tom Prink did it with planning and precision. If they think you're getting close..." She doesn't finish the sentence, but the implication hangs in the air between us.

"Don't worry," I assure her, reaching down to pat Joe's massive head. "I've got two hundred and fifty pounds of canine security detail and a Maggie. I'll be fine."

But as Officer Basilier leaves and we prepare to track down our tearful actress, I can't help wondering if I've just volunteered to be the next target in someone's carefully orchestrated production. After all, what's a Shakespearean tragedy without a growing body count?

I'VE SPENT SO much time in this dusty old theatre that it's starting to smell like home. Lighting rigs and pulley systems hover overhead, exposed like an anatomy lesson. The smell of fresh paint and wood shavings wafts through the air. As Maggie, Joe, and I make our way down the center aisle, a single figure stands on the empty stage, her voice rising and falling in the practiced cadence of a Shakespearean soliloquy. Monica Blanchart, arms outstretched toward the vacant seats, transforms before our eyes from the timid, stuttering woman we met days ago into Katherina the shrew, fierce and commanding. It's like watching a butterfly emerge from a cocoon, except this metamorphosis happens in reverse— the moment she notices us, her voice falters, arms drop, and she shrinks back into herself, becoming small again.

"Oh! I d-didn't realize anyone was... I was just..." Monica's hands flutter nervously at her sides like wounded birds. She takes a small step back, as if trying to disappear into the scenery.

"Please, don't stop on our account," I call up to her. "That was incredible."

Joe lets out a soft woof of agreement, his tail sweeping

across the dusty floor as he watches Monica with what I can only describe as canine appreciation for the dramatic arts.

"We were hoping to talk to you for a few minutes," Maggie adds, already pulling out her notebook. "About Tom, and the production."

"*And* your recent commitment to social activism for the arts," I add, unable to keep the edge out of my voice. Then, I clarify: "We saw your testimonial on the *Restart the Shrew* website."

Monica's eyes immediately fill with tears. Not the single, perfectly timed tear from her video testimonial, but a sudden flood that transforms her face into a glistening mask of grief. The speed of this emotional shift is almost alarming.

"It's such a difficult situation," she says, her voice catching. "I hope you know that, Rebecca."

"The correct way to address Rebecca, for those that don't know her well, is 'Your Grace,'" Maggie bristles.

"Of course!" Monica says, one hand flying over her mouth at the social faux pas she just committed. "I apologize, Your Grace," she turns back to me. "I'm afraid I'm quite rattled by everything. I just love the arts so much. And I'm absolutely shattered about Tom. Let's talk," she adds magnanimously. "Why don't you join me?"

She gestures for us to join her on stage, and we climb the small set of steps at the side. Joe follows with the dignified caution of a dog who understands that stages are inherently suspicious places where floors sometimes move and strange noises happen without warning.

Up close, Monica looks exhausted. Dark circles shadow her eyes despite an attempt to cover them with makeup. Her hands tremble as she brushes hair from her face. She sits on the edge of a wooden bench that's part of the set, patting the space beside her in invitation.

"Thank you for agreeing to talk with us," I say, settling next to her while Maggie pulls over a chair. Joe remains standing, his watchful gaze moving between Monica and the backstage area, as if he's appointed himself our security detail. "I have to say, your public video surprised me. I think I've been really open with everyone. If you wanted the play reopened, you could have talked to me personally rather than attacking me online."

Fresh tears spill down Monica's cheeks. "Jenny asked us all to record something," she explains, wiping at her face with the sleeve of her cardigan. "I didn't want to, but she said it was important for the cast to show a united front."

"Well you did a great job," Maggie adds, her tone sarcastic. "It was very moving."

Monica flushes slightly. "I'm only comfortable when I'm being someone else," she admits. "As Katherina, or any character, really. When it's just me, Monica, I feel like I don't know what to say or how to be." Her voice drops to a whisper. "Jenny had to do seventeen takes. I kept freezing up."

That explains some of the inconsistency, but not all of it. There's something almost performative about her grief.

"You mentioned in the video that Tom was kind to you," I prompt. "That he helped you with your lines?"

The dam breaks. Monica's quiet tears transform into heaving sobs that shake her small frame. "He was the only one who took time to help me," she chokes out between gasps. "When I would f-freeze up at rehearsal, everyone else would get impatient, but T-Tom would just smile and say, 'Let's try again, Monica. You've got this.'"

Joe, sensing her distress, moves closer and rests his massive head on the edge of the bench near her hand. Monica absently strokes his fur as she struggles to compose herself.

"I'm sorry," she says after a moment, wiping her face. "It's just— without this production, I don't know what I'll do. My apartment... I won't be able to make rent next month if the show doesn't go on."

"The play is your only source of income?" Maggie asks, her pen hovering over her notebook.

Monica nods miserably. "I was on a soap opera for a while — 'Days of Monrovia'— but my character was killed off three months ago. This role was supposed to be my comeback." She laughs bitterly through her tears. "My agent said it would 'remind people I exist.' Now Tom is dead, and I might be homeless by Christmas."

The financial motive registers in both Maggie's and my expression, though we try to hide it. Money is one of the oldest motives for murder, and Monica has just handed us a clear reason why she might have wanted to draw more attention to the play through murder.

"It must look awful to you," I say, realizing something. "Here I am refusing to restart the play while I live in a big castle and don't have to worry about a thing."

"Well–" Monica says, blushing. "No, I don't– I didn't think–"

"It's okay," I say, nodding. "You're right. I *didn't* think about how long you all could go without a paycheck. I'm sorry."

Monica's mouth drops open as she takes in the apology. "Royalty doesn't usually talk like this," she says.

"I'm not Royalty," I shrug. "Just someone who doesn't want to see anyone else hurt. I was afraid to restart the play because the murderer is still out there. I didn't want anyone else to get hurt."

Monica shakes her head, fresh tears welling. "That's what scares me the most," she whispers. "What if it's someone in the cast? What if we're all rehearsing with a... a murderer?" Her voice breaks on the last word.

"You must have theories," Maggie presses. "Observations about who might have had conflicts with Tom, or who behaved strangely that night."

"Everyone was normal," Monica insists, sniffling. "Just

pre-show nerves. Tom was excited about his family coming to opening night. He kept checking his phone for texts from his mother."

"What about Brent Thoroughgood?" Maggie asks, her tone deliberately casual. "We've heard he can be... demanding. Did he and Tom ever clash?"

At the mention of Brent, something shifts in Monica's expression— subtle but unmistakable. A tightening around the eyes, a slight flush creeping up her neck.

"Brent is intense," she admits, "but he wouldn't hurt anyone. He takes his craft seriously, that's all."

"His 'craft,'" I repeat, unable to keep a hint of skepticism from my voice. "Including making his brother understudy for a role he clearly isn't ready for?"

Monica's eyes dart away, focusing on Joe instead of meeting my gaze. "Josh is... struggling," she acknowledges. "But Brent just wants to help him. Family is important to Brent."

There's a weightiness to the way she says "family" that makes me wonder if there's more to that story. I exchange a quick glance with Maggie, who gives an almost imperceptible nod. She's caught it too.

"You seem to know Brent quite well," Maggie observes. "Have you worked together before?"

Monica's blush deepens. "No, just this production. But he's been very supportive of my performance. He says I have real talent." She touches her throat nervously, fingers playing with a delicate silver necklace I hadn't noticed before. A small "B" charm dangles from the chain.

Well, that's interesting. And potentially very relevant.

"Monica," I say carefully, "is there something between you and Brent that might be important for us to know about?"

She looks up, panic flashing in her tear-swollen eyes. "No! I mean, we've become friends during rehearsals, that's all." The denial is too quick, too forceful to be convincing. "Brent is just naturally charming with everyone. Ask anyone in the cast."

Before we can push further, the sound of a door opening backstage catches everyone's attention. Monica jumps to her feet like a startled deer.

"I should get back to rehearsing," she says hurriedly, gathering her script. "Jenny wants us to run through Act Three again before lunch." She takes a few steps away, then turns back, her face a mask of renewed grief, tears flowing on cue. "Please find who did this to Tom. He deserved so much better. And I'm sorry, Rebe– I mean, Your *Grace*– about the video. Really."

As Monica disappears backstage, Joe lets out a soft whine, as if expressing his own skepticism about her performance.

"Well," Maggie says once Monica is safely out of earshot, "that was..."

"Broadway-worthy," I finish for her. "Especially the quick transition from 'potential romantic involvement with our prime suspect' to 'grieving colleague concerned only with justice.'"

"Do you think the tears were real?" Maggie asks, flipping through her notes.

"Some of them," I decide after a moment's thought. "The financial panic seemed genuine. The rest..." I shrug. "Let's just say if the acting thing doesn't work out, she has a promising future in courtroom testimonials. And that necklace she was wearing had a letter B on it. Do you think she could be dating Brent?"

Joe noses my hand, his expression somehow managing to convey that he agrees with my assessment. Sometimes I think he's a better judge of character than I am.

"Definitely," Maggie says, lowering her voice, "So we've got a weepy actress who might be romantically involved with Brent Thoroughgood and who *definitely* needs this play to continue for financial reasons."

"She can turn the waterworks on and off faster than a faulty bathroom faucet," I add. "She's still on our list of suspects. And now, she's higher than before. If she's in love with Brent, maybe she thought she was helping him by killing Tom."

———

As Maggie and I step down from the stage, Joe trotting faithfully beside us, I'm already mentally organizing our suspect list. Monica has catapulted toward the top with her financial motive and possible relationship with Brent, though something about her grief feels genuine beneath all the theatrical flourish. It's like trying to find a real diamond mixed in with excellent fakes— they all catch the light just right, but only one has the substance to cut glass. I'm so lost in these thoughts that I nearly collide with Jenny Jay, who materializes in front of us with the sudden appearance of a jack-in-the-box, today's pleated skirt adorned with tiny embroidered peacocks that seem to stare accusingly at me.

"Your Grace!" Jenny exclaims, her voice pitched with the kind of theatrical enthusiasm that probably carries to the back row without a microphone. "I was hoping to catch you before you left!"

Joe lets out a low rumble that isn't quite a growl but definitely communicates his opinion of Jenny's ambush tactics. I place a calming hand on his massive head, silently thanking him for his canine intuition while simultaneously asking him to dial it back.

"Jenny," I acknowledge with a polite nod. "We were just finishing up a conversation with Monica."

"Wonderful, wonderful!" Jenny claps her hands together, the sound echoing in the empty theater. "Monica is such a talent, isn't she? So raw, so emotionally available. That's why I cast her." She leans forward conspiratorially. "Her video testimonial has the most shares on social media, you know. Over ten thousand! People are absolutely devastated by her grief."

"Speaking of the video testimonials," Maggie interjects smoothly, "that's quite a professional website you've put together. In such a short time, too."

Jenny's smile doesn't falter, but something flickers in her eyes— pride mixed with the briefest flash of wariness. "Oh, you've seen it? Yes, we had a... a template ready for promotional purposes before the tragedy. I simply repurposed it. One must be adaptable in this industry."

"Very adaptable," I agree, carefully neutral. "Those petition signatures are impressive."

"Aren't they?" Jenny beams, her face lighting up like she's accepting an award. "Over three thousand now! The community is absolutely rallying behind us. Local businesses have even started offering discounts to anyone who shows proof they've signed." She pulls her phone from the pocket of her garishly yellow cardigan, tapping rapidly at the screen. "Here, let me show you some of the comments people have left. They're desperate for the show to go on."

Before I can politely decline, Jenny thrusts her phone into my hands. The screen displays a seemingly endless scroll of comments, ranging from heartfelt tributes to Tom (mostly from people who clearly never met him) to passionate defenses of art in the face of tragedy. One comment catches my eye: "The Duchess must understand that art transcends death! #RestartTheShrew #DuchessOfDeath"

I hand the phone back, forcing a smile. "You've certainly mobilized public opinion."

"The question," Jenny says, leaning forward with an intensity that makes Joe shift protectively closer to my side, "is whether it's had any impact on your decision. The cast is ready. We've continued rehearsals, honoring Tom through our dedication to the craft." She clasps her hands together, pressing them to her heart. "Please, Your Grace. Allow us to open this Saturday. We've already sold out, with proceeds now going to a memorial scholarship in Tom's name."

I'm about to ask how they're selling tickets to a show that hasn't been officially approved when I remember Officer Basilier's suggestion: *Use the performance to flush out the killer. Let them think they've gotten away with it, then watch for nervous behavior or another attempt.*

"You know what, Jenny?" I say, making my decision. "I think restarting the production is *exactly* the right move."

Jenny freezes, her mouth half-open in what was clearly going to be another impassioned plea. "You... you do?"

"Absolutely!" I say with conviction that grows as I speak. "Tom wouldn't want this play– filled with people he cared about– to go unseen. The show should open this Saturday, as hoped."

Jenny's face transforms, the surprise giving way to triumphant joy that she doesn't even try to temper with appropriate solemnity. "Oh, Your Grace! This is— I mean— the entire company will be so grateful! I knew you would understand the cultural significance of— "

"I understand more than you think," I cut in smoothly. "Theater is about truth, isn't it? Revealing what's hidden. I think this production might reveal quite a lot."

Something in my tone makes Jenny's smile falter momentarily, but she recovers quickly. "Absolutely! Truth! That's exactly what Shakespeare is all about!" She takes a step back, already mentally shifting to her director mode. "I should tell the cast immediately. We'll need to run a full dress rehearsal tomorrow, and the lighting cues still need work, and—"

"YOU CAN'T!"

The voice echoes through the theater, raw with panic. We all turn to see Josh Thoroughgood stumbling down the center aisle, his face ashen, script clutched in a white-knuckled grip. He looks like he's been running, his hair wild, clothes rumpled as if he's been sleeping in them.

"Josh," Jenny hisses, her smile instantly replaced by irritation. "We're in the middle of an important conversation with the Duchess. Perhaps you could—"

"No!" Josh shouts, reaching the edge of the stage and clambering up the steps with none of his brother's grace. "No, you can't restart the show. It's not safe!" He turns to me, eyes wide with genuine terror. "Your Grace, please. You can't let this continue."

"Josh, you're being ridiculous," Jenny snaps, all pretense of artistic camaraderie evaporating. "Go back to rehearsal. NOW."

But Josh ignores her, advancing toward me with a desperation that makes Joe move partially in front of my legs, a living barrier of protective fur. "You don't understand," Josh pleads, his voice cracking. "Bad things happen in this theater. Tom wasn't an accident. And if you start the show again—" He chokes on the words, tears welling in his eyes.

"If I start the show again, what?" I prompt, keeping my voice gentle despite the tension prickling along my spine.

"People will die!" Josh bursts out. His hands shake as he runs them through his already disheveled hair. "Don't you get it? There's a reason I can't remember a single line. This production is cursed or haunted or something. Tom was just the beginning."

Jenny makes a disgusted sound. "For heaven's sake, Josh! Pull yourself together! You're embarrassing yourself and insulting the memory of a colleague."

"I don't care!" Josh shouts back, his voice rising to a pitch that makes me wince. "I can't do this anymore. I won't!" He turns back to me, suddenly looking less frightened and more determined. "If you start it again, I'll make sure it's shut down! I'll go to the press. I'll tell them everything!"

"Tell them what, exactly?" Maggie asks, her pen poised over her notebook.

Josh opens his mouth to answer, but whatever revelation he's about to make is cut short by a sickening crack from overhead. I glance up just in time to see a heavy stage light breaking free from its mounting, plummeting toward us with terrifying speed.

"Josh!" I shout, lunging forward. Beside me, Joe– my constant guardian– bites at the leg of my pants to hold me back, keeping me from moving toward the crashing light fixture. His choice saves me, but it dooms Josh– I'm just a second too late to push him out of the way.

With a crash, the light descends from overhead, falling in slow motion. Glass shatters. Someone screams. I can just make out Josh's limp form crumpling under a mess of twisted metal. He's a marionette with cut strings, the script fluttering from his hand like a wounded bird.

For a moment, the entire theatre falls into silence. I look down at my dog, who just saved my life. He's staring up at me with concerned eyes, as if he's asking *"Are you still here?"* I reach down and take his face in my hands. "Thank you," I whisper.

"Oh my God!" Jenny shrieks, stumbling backward. "Oh my God, oh my God!"

I tell Joe to sit, then step forward toward the metal light fixture that's covering Josh's limp form. I drop to my knees beside him, heart hammering. Blood seeps from a gash on his temple, but he's breathing, his pulse rapid but steady under my fingers.

"Call an ambulance," I tell Maggie, who already has her phone out. "And Officer Basilier. This wasn't an accident."

"He's alive?" Jenny asks, keeping her distance as if Josh's unconscious body might somehow implicate her.

"For now," I say grimly. I turn to Maggie. "Stay with him until help arrives."

Maggie nods, her face pale but composed as she speaks urgently into her phone. Joe nudges my arm, his eyes fixed on the catwalks and lighting rigs above us. He lets out a soft whine, then turns his gaze toward the backstage area.

"You're right, buddy," I whisper, rising to my feet. "Someone had to be up there. Let's go."

Without waiting for Jenny's reaction, Joe and I race toward the wings, taking the narrow metal stairs two at a time. My heart pounds in my ears as we reach the upper level where technicians operate the lighting and scenery. The catwalk is narrow, suspended high above the stage, with just a thin railing between the walkway and a thirty-foot drop.

"Hello?" I call out, scanning the dim space. "Anyone here?"

Only silence answers, but Joe's nose works overtime, sniffing along the metal grating. He stops at a specific point, looking up at me with meaningful eyes. I follow his gaze to a control panel where a thick rope dangles, swaying slightly in the air current from a nearby vent. The frayed end shows where it was recently cut.

"Someone did this on purpose," I murmur, examining the rope without touching it. "Someone who knew exactly which rope to cut, and which light was positioned above Josh."

Joe whines softly, moving back toward the stairs with purpose.

"You're right," I agree, following him. "We need to get back to your Aunt Maggie. Whoever did this might not be done yet."

As we descend the stairs, a chilling thought occurs to me: Josh said he would tell "everything" if the play continued. Now he can't tell anyone anything— at least not until he regains consciousness. *If* he regains consciousness.

What exactly does Josh know? And more importantly, who was so desperate to silence him that they'd risk getting caught?

The answer, I suspect, is somewhere in this theater, perhaps watching us even now from the shadows, waiting to see what we'll do next in this increasingly deadly production.

CHAPTER
Sixteen

HOSPITAL WAITING rooms always smell like disinfectant. I've visited enough of them in my animal training career to recognize the particular blend of antiseptic chemicals, stale coffee, and quiet dread that hangs in the air. Joe sits pressed against my leg, his warm bulk providing the only comfort in this sterile purgatory as we wait for news about Josh Thoroughgood. His massive head swivels periodically toward the double doors where doctors occasionally emerge with news for other anxious families, but so far, nothing for us. I keep replaying the sickening crack of that light breaking free, the horrifying moment when it struck Josh mid-sentence, silencing whatever revelation he was about to share.

"You should eat something," Maggie says, pushing a wrapped sandwich toward me. "It's been four hours."

"I'm not hungry," I reply, though my stomach immediately betrays me with an audible growl. "Fine. My stomach's a traitor."

I unwrap the sandwich without enthusiasm, taking a mechanical bite of what turns out to be turkey and cheese. It tastes like nothing, just texture in my mouth. Joe watches me eat with the focused attention of a dog who believes sharing is the cornerstone of a healthy human-canine relationship.

"Sorry, buddy," I whisper. "Hospital food is questionable enough for humans. I'm not subjecting your digestive system to it."

The automatic doors at the entrance slide open, and Jack hurries in with Luma trotting beside him. His face is tight with worry, tie slightly askew— a rare lapse in ducal perfection that speaks volumes about his concern. Luma spots Joe immediately and pulls toward him, her leash stretching taut before Jack releases it.

"Rebecca," Jack says, crossing the waiting room in four long strides. He takes the seat beside me, his hand finding mine with gentle pressure. "I came as soon as I could get away from the agricultural minister. Are you all right? Were you hurt?"

"I'm fine," I assure him. "Not even a scratch. But Josh..." I trail off, glancing toward those implacable double doors again.

"You said someone deliberately cut the rigging?" Jack keeps his voice low, mindful of the other people scattered around the waiting area.

I nod. "Joe and I found where the rope had been sabotaged. It wasn't an accident. Someone wanted to silence Josh before he could tell us whatever he knew."

At our feet, Joe and Luma have settled into a familiar greeting ritual— Luma circling Joe once, then pressing against his side, both dogs sighing in unison like old friends reuniting after a long separation. Their uncomplicated canine affection makes my throat tighten unexpectedly.

"Officer Basilier's forensics team was still processing the scene when I left," Maggie explains, closing her tablet where she's been making notes. "They're checking for fingerprints, fibers, anything that might identify who was up in the rigging. But so far, nothing..." She shrugs, the gesture eloquently conveying the frustration we all feel.

"What happened after I ran upstairs?" I ask, suddenly realizing I don't know how Josh got from the stage to the hospital.

"Jenny completely lost it," Maggie says, tucking a strand of blonde hair behind her ear. "Started screaming about curses and insurance premiums in the same breath. Cosmo came out from the wings and stayed with Josh while I called the ambulance. The paramedics arrived within minutes."

"And Jenny?"

"Jenny disappeared shortly after the ambulance left," Maggie says, her expression darkening. "Claimed she needed to 'manage the situation with the cast.' I tried to insist she stay to give a statement to Officer Basilier, but she was out the door before I could stop her."

"Convenient," I mutter.

"Very," Maggie agrees. "Almost as convenient as the timing of that lighting 'accident.'"

The waiting room doors swing open again, and Officer Basilier strides in, her uniform impeccably pressed despite what must have been hours of overseeing the crime scene. Joe immediately sits up straighter, as if preparing for an official police briefing. Even Luma assumes a more dignified posture.

We all tense, waiting for news— good or bad. Hospital updates have this terrible binary quality. There's rarely an in-between.

"Orange," Officer Basilier nods to me, then acknowledges the others. "Duke. Lefevere. Assorted canines."

"How is he?" I ask, not bothering with pleasantries.

"Broken leg, concussion, twelve stitches in his scalp," Officer Basilier reports with clinical efficiency. "But he'll live. He's conscious and coherent— or as coherent as he ever was."

The relief that floods through me is surprisingly intense. I hadn't realized how worried I was until the worry evaporated.

"Thank God," Jack murmurs beside me.

"Can we see him?" Maggie asks.

"Not yet. Doctors are still running tests, and we've posted an officer outside his room. His brother, Brent, is by his bedside, and currently threatening to sue everyone. Hope the castle has good lawyers, Orange." Officer Basilier drops into the chair across from us, her usual rigid posture relaxing fractionally. It's the closest thing to exhaustion I've ever seen from her. "I've questioned Josh already. Says he has no idea who would want to hurt him."

"He's lying," I say immediately. "You didn't see how panicked he was, how desperate to stop the production. He was about to tell us something important when that light fell."

"I agree," Officer Basilier says, surprising me with the easy acknowledgment. "But without him coming clean, we're stuck playing this cat-and-mouse game with our killer."

"Did forensics find anything in the rigging?" Maggie asks.

"Nothing useful. Whoever did it wore gloves, and the catwalk is used by multiple crew members throughout the day. Too many overlapping prints and fibers to isolate anything conclusive." Officer Basilier shakes her head in frustration. "We're back to square one, unless Josh decides to start talking."

"So what happens now?" Jack asks, his thumb tracing small circles on the back of my hand. It's a gesture so subtle no one else would notice, but it steadies me, grounds me.

"Now we decide whether to proceed with the reopening," Officer Basilier says, looking directly at me. "It's ultimately your call, Your Grace, but my recommendation hasn't changed. I still think our best chance of catching this killer is to let the show go on and watch for suspicious behavior."

"Even after *this*?" I gesture toward the hospital corridors where Josh lies injured. "Someone's escalating from poison to dropping lighting equipment. What if they try something during the actual performance?"

"That's exactly what we're hoping for," Officer Basilier says grimly. "Except this time, we'll be ready. I'm assigning plain-clothes officers throughout the audience and backstage. We'll have officers monitoring all entrances and exits."

"It's our best chance," Maggie agrees quietly. "As terrible as it sounds, we need to create an opportunity for the killer to act again."

"But with safeguards in place," Jack adds, his protective instincts clearly engaged. "I won't have Rebecca put at risk."

"I think we should proceed," I decide. "The opening should continue as planned this Saturday. We'll announce that Josh's injury was an unfortunate accident, that he's expected to make a full recovery, and that the production will continue with his understudy." I pause, realizing the flaw in this plan. "Does Josh even have an understudy? He was already an understudy himself."

"That's the theater business for you," Maggie says with a small smile. "Everyone's always one accident away from their big break. According to the program, Josh's understudy is someone named Ellis Porter. Cosmo says he's been at every rehearsal, taking notes. He's apparently ready to step in."

"How convenient," Officer Basilier mutters. "Is there anyone who *doesn't* have a motive for murder in this play?!"

"It feels like we're getting close," I say, the conviction growing as I speak. "The killer is getting nervous, making mistakes. First Tom, now Josh— the killer feels cornered, which means we're doing our jobs."

"I agree," Officer Basilier says, and I blink in surprise at this second easy concession from her. "You've got good instincts, Orange. Better than half my department, though I'll deny saying that if you ever repeat it."

"Me? Good instincts?" I place a hand over my heart in mock astonishment. "Officer Basilier, are you feeling well?

Should we call a doctor? You're being suspiciously complimentary."

A rare smile flickers across her face. "Don't get used to it. I still think your methods are unorthodox at best and completely reckless at worst. But..." she sighs, as if the admission pains her, "I'm glad to have someone untameable like you on this case, even if you do drive me crazy."

"I have that effect on authority figures," I say with a grin. "You and Mrs. Trechón are at the top of my 'people I drive crazy' list."

Officer Basilier waves a dismissive hand. "Mrs. Trechón will have to come to terms with your wild ways, just like I have. You'll either befriend her or make her absolutely furious by the end of all this. There's no in-between."

Jack squeezes my hand gently, drawing my attention back to him. "I'm proud of you," he says softly, his eyes warm with affection. "Most people in your position would distance themselves from this whole mess, let the police handle it and protect their reputation. But you're diving in headfirst because it's the right thing to do."

"You married an animal trainer, not a proper duchess," I remind him with a small smile. "Getting my hands dirty is kind of my specialty."

"And when this investigation is done," he continues, "we're going on that honeymoon. No murders, no duchessing, no Mrs. Trechón. Just us."

The promise of that escape— sunshine, privacy, no one critiquing my curtsy technique or suspecting me of harboring criminal tendencies— feels almost too good to be true. But before we can get there, I need one more piece of this puzzle.

"I'll hold you to that," I tell him. "But I need one favor from you before then."

Jack raises an eyebrow, curious. "Anything."

"I need the Queen's phone number."

His other eyebrow joins the first in surprise. "The Queen? My aunt? You've finally decided to call her about–"

"I have," I smile. "Mrs. Trechón was sent specifically to 'help' me adjust to being a duchess. In a very unexpected way, she's done a fine job. I'm ready to speak to the Queen, all on my own."

Jack studies me for a long moment, then nods slowly. "I'll get you her private number." Jack laughs softly. "She calls you 'the animal enthusiast.' Actually, I think she rather likes that you're different."

"Perfect," I say with more confidence than I feel. "Then she shouldn't mind answering a few questions from her newest duchess."

Officer Basilier clears her throat. "While you're plotting royal phone calls, I need to get back to the station. We have a press statement to prepare about continuing the production." She stands, straightening her already immaculate uniform. "I'll be in touch about security arrangements for Saturday."

As we gather our things to leave— the doctors have made it clear we won't be seeing Josh tonight—I feel a strange mix of dread and anticipation. Saturday's opening night is both a trap we're setting and one we might be walking into. But for the first time since this investigation began, I feel like we're pushing the killer to make a mistake instead of just reacting to their moves.

Joe stands and stretches, his massive body extending to its full impressive length before he shakes himself from head to tail. Luma watches this display with what I can only describe as fond exasperation—the same look Jack often gives me when I'm being particularly stubborn.

"Ready to catch a killer?" I ask Joe as I clip his leash to his collar.

He responds with a soft woof that manages to convey both "absolutely" and "can we get real food on the way home?" in a single canine syllable.

Some questions don't require a royal consultation to answer. "Yes," I tell him. "We're definitely stopping for croissants."

His tail wags with such enthusiasm that a nearby potted plant trembles in fear. At least someone's priorities remain uncomplicated, even as the rest of us prepare to enter the final act of this increasingly dangerous production.

CHAPTER
Seventeen

THE MONROVIAN ROYAL Theater glows like a jewel box against the evening sky, its façade illuminated by floodlights that make the century-old stonework seem alive with possibility. I stand at the entrance, one hand clutching my unnecessarily formal clutch purse, the other resting on Joe's massive head as he sits regally beside me in his custom-made "formal" collar— a ridiculous confection of black satin and tiny rhinestones that he tolerates with surprising dignity. Benjamin had it designed just for Joe, and he didn't hold back on the bling. Inside this building, a murderer might be preparing for their final act, but out here, it's all champagne, evening gowns, and the usual tension of opening night. *Well, in this case, "second" opening night.*

"Are you ready?" Jack asks, offering his arm with a smile that still makes my heart do a little flip, even after all these months. He looks impossibly handsome in his formal attire, the kind of duke that fairy tales promise but reality rarely delivers.

"As ready as I'll ever be to attend a play where two people have already been attacked," I reply, slipping my hand into the crook of his elbow. "Let's just hope our trap works and nobody else gets hurt."

"Maybe we'll actually get to see the play this time," Jack agrees.

Behind us, Officer Basilier adjusts her simple evening gown, which I'm certain conceals at least three weapons and possibly a small tactical radio. Her expression remains professionally neutral, but I catch the slight narrowing of her eyes as she scans the arriving guests.

"My officers are in position," she says quietly. "Four in the audience, two backstage, one at each exit. If our killer makes a move tonight, we'll be ready."

Maggie appears beside us, resplendent in a midnight blue dress that complements her blonde braids, now elegantly coiled atop her head. "The press is already inside," she warns. "They've been told you'll give a brief statement before the performance."

"Wonderful," I mutter. "Nothing I love more than talking to reporters while trying to catch a murderer."

Luma trots up to us, a matching formal collar around her neck making her look like Joe's sophisticated date to a canine gala. She's just been set loose by Benjamin, who was fitting her with her own custom formal-wear. Benjamin waves at me and gives me a thumbs-up as Luma licks Joe's face fondly. The two dogs exchange what I swear is a knowing look— the kind shared by reluctant attendees at formal events everywhere.

"Your Grace!" The voice cuts through the pleasant murmur of arriving theatergoers like a knife through butter. Mrs. Trechón approaches with military precision, her steel-gray dress as rigid and unyielding as her personality. "We must proceed immediately to the press area. They're expecting your statement about supporting the arts in Monrovia. I've prepared some appropriate remarks for you, given that I'm sure whatever *you'd* plan to say on your own would only create more trouble."

She holds out a small card with what I assume are meticulously scripted, perfectly proper platitudes that any "real" duchess would deliver with practiced grace.

"Actually," I say, handing the card back without looking at it, "I won't be speaking to the press yet. I'm going backstage first to wish the actors well."

Mrs. Trechón's face freezes in a mask of polite horror. "Backstage? Before a performance? That's highly irregular, Your Grace. The protocol clearly states—"

"I'm not particularly concerned with protocol tonight," I interrupt, maintaining a smile for the benefit of nearby guests. "As the patron of this theater, I feel it's important to show personal support for the cast, especially after what they've been through."

"But the press—" Mrs. Trechón begins.

"Will still be there after I've spoken with the actors," I finish for her.

Her nostrils flare slightly, a warning sign I've come to recognize as preceding one of her lectures. "Your Grace, I must insist. There are traditions that must be maintained. The dignity of your position—"

"Mrs. Trechón," I say, my patience finally evaporating like morning dew on a hot day. "Do you know what I learned in my years working with wild animals?"

The unexpected question throws her off balance. "I... what?"

"I learned that some creatures simply can't be tamed," I continue, meeting her gaze directly. "You can train them, you can build mutual respect, you can establish boundaries— but you can never break their essential nature. And if you try, you'll only damage what makes them special in the first place."

Understanding dawns in her eyes. "And you believe you are one such... creature?"

"I *know* I am," I reply without hesitation. "Just like Katherina in *Taming of the Shrew*. You can try to force me into a mold, but in the end, I'll always be fundamentally myself."

"Katherina offers a speech of acquiesence at the end of the play," Mrs. Trechón says in a terse voice. "If you knew anything about Shakespeare–"

"Actually," Jack clears his throat. "I was taught that her speech is delivered quite sarcastically. And I think you'll agree I had the best tutors, no?"

Mrs. Trechón's lips press into a thin line.

"Katherina wasn't tamed," I say, standing a little straighter. "She only learned how to persevere in a difficult world by pretending to give the people what they wanted. Just like me."

"This is unacceptable!" Mrs. Trechón says, practically pulling her hair out. Her cheeks flush a bright crimson color. "I will have to contact Her Majesty about this continued defiance. The Queen will—"

"The Queen already knows how I feel," I interrupt gently. "I spoke with her yesterday."

Mrs. Trechón blinks rapidly, genuinely shocked for perhaps the first time since I've known her. "You... contacted Her Majesty? Directly?"

"I did." I can't help but smile at the memory of that conversation— the Queen's unexpected warmth, her surprising laugh when I admitted how terrified I was to call her. "We had quite a lovely chat about what it means to be a duchess in the modern world. About blending tradition with progress. About finding one's own path while respecting the institution. And about our opinions of Katherina in *Taming of the Shrew*."

"And she... agreed with your perspective?" Mrs. Trechón asks, her voice faint with disbelief.

"She said the monarchy has survived for centuries precisely because it evolves," I tell her, softening my tone. "She also said that some of the most valuable members of the royal family through history were those who initially seemed the least suitable. She told me she often feels like Katherina herself– playing a role in the show that is life. We bonded over the idea."

Mrs. Trechón's shoulders slump almost imperceptibly, the rigid perfection of her posture faltering for just a moment. In that brief window of vulnerability, I glimpse the woman behind the façade— the one whose dreams of royalty were shattered decades ago, leaving her with nothing but rules and protocols to cling to.

"Mrs. Trechón," I say carefully, "I think it's time we both acknowledge that this arrangement isn't working for either of us. You deserve a position where your considerable skills and knowledge are truly appreciated, not wasted on someone who resists them at every turn."

"You're... dismissing me?" she asks, her voice carefully controlled.

"I'm setting you free," I correct her. "Just because being royal wasn't your destiny doesn't mean there isn't something wonderful waiting for you. The Queen mentioned the Royal Historical Society is looking for someone with your expertise in court etiquette and traditions. They need someone to catalog and preserve centuries of protocol that might other-wise be lost."

Something flickers in her eyes— a spark of interest that breaks through her mask of disappointment.

"The Queen suggested this position... for me?" she asks.

"She thought it would be perfect," I confirm. "Your knowl-edge wouldn't just be tolerated there— it would be valued. Celebrated, even."

Mrs. Trechón stands silent for a long moment, processing this unexpected turn of events. For a moment, I expect her to yell at me or break down crying. There's a wild look in her eyes, and her hair seems to deflate a little, crazy tendrils coming loose from their tightly coiled cage. I think about the vision board in her bedroom, and how she's dedicated her life to the monarchy. *Is she going to scream at me?*

But when she finally speaks, her voice holds a note I've never heard before— something approaching gratitude.

"That is... most considerate of you, Your Grace." She straightens her already immaculate posture. Her right hand floats up to her hair, tucking the loose pieces back in place where they belong. "I shall consider Her Majesty's suggestion most carefully."

"I think you'll find it suits you," I tell her with genuine warmth. "You have passion, Mrs. Trechón. It deserves to be directed somewhere it can truly flourish."

Something that might almost be a smile touches the corners of her mouth. "Perhaps you're right." She inclines her head slightly, a gesture that feels like the closest thing to approval she's ever offered me. "I wish you good fortune with your... unconventional approach to duchessing. The way you handled this confrontation with me, well– perhaps it shows you know more about being a royal than I've recognized."

"Thank you," I say, surprised by how much her quasi-blessing means to me. "And I wish you happiness in whatever comes next."

As Mrs. Trechón turns and walks away with characteristic precision, I feel a weight lift from my shoulders that I hadn't fully acknowledged until its absence.

"Did that really just happen?" Maggie whispers, appearing at my side. "Did you just fire Mrs. Trechón and have her thank you for it?"

"I think I just helped her find her true calling," I reply, watching Mrs. Trechón disappear into the crowd. "Besides, now I can focus on what really matters tonight— catching our killer."

Jack squeezes my hand gently. "Are you ready to go back-stage? The show starts in twenty minutes."

"Absolutely," I say, squaring my shoulders. "Let's see if we can spot any nervous behavior among our suspects."

As we make our way toward the stage door, Joe and Luma padding faithfully beside us, I feel the familiar rush of adrenaline that comes with closing in on a mystery. Tonight, I'll either catch a murderer or give them the perfect opportunity to strike again. Either way, the final act is about to begin.

———

The backstage area of a theater on opening night has its own particular energy— part panic, part prayer, part superstitious ritual. As Joe and I navigate the narrow corridor leading from the stage door to the green room, we pass crew members frozen in various attitudes of last-minute crisis management. A seamstress frantically sews something sparkly, her fingers moving with blur-like speed; a man balances precariously on a ladder, adjusting a light that probably won't be fixed in time; two stage hands whisper-argue about the proper place-ment of a chair that seems, to my untrained eye, to be exactly where it should be. The smell of greasepaint and anxiety hangs heavy in the air, a combination that reminds me oddly of the big cat enclosure before feeding time— predatory antic-ipation tinged with the knowledge that something dramatic is about to occur.

Joe walks silently beside me, his enormous presence causing several stagehands to flatten themselves against walls to let us pass. I've left Officer Basilier, Maggie, and the dogs in the lobby— this is a mission I need to handle alone, with only my furry lie detector at my side.

We find the cast gathered in the green room, a space that manages to feel simultaneously cramped and cavernous. Jenny Jay paces in tight circles, today's pleated skirt adorned with tiny embroidered theater masks that seem to watch us as she moves. Monica sits apart from the others, her transformation into Katherina already beginning—her posture straighter, her gaze more direct than the shy woman we interviewed days ago. Brent Thoroughgood stands before a mirror, not checking his makeup but simply admiring his own reflection with the self-assured complacency of someone who's never questioned their place in the universe. Shockingly, Josh– only recently out of the hospital– huddles in a corner chair, his bandaged leg propped awkwardly before him, script clutched in trembling hands as his lips move in silent recitation of lines he still hasn't mastered.

They're still having Josh perform? I think to myself, horrified. *These people really mean it when they say the show must go on.*

In the background, Cosmo flits about like a nervous moth, adjusting props, checking lights, his mustache drooping with the weight of his multiple responsibilities. His movements have the frantic quality of someone responsible for too many tasks and possessing too little time.

"Your Grace!" Jenny exclaims when she notices me, her voice climbing to a pitch that makes Joe's ears twitch in protest. "What a delightful surprise! We weren't expecting you backstage before the performance!"

The sudden attention makes everyone freeze, creating a tableau of theatrical anxiety interrupted. All eyes turn to me, some curious, some wary, all wondering why the Duchess of Atwood has appeared in their sanctuary minutes before the curtain rises.

"I wanted to wish you all good luck personally," I say, finding my duchess voice—the one that's authoritative yet warm, formal yet authentic. "This production has overcome significant challenges, and your perseverance deserves recognition."

Jenny beams, practically vibrating with the validation.

"How extraordinarily thoughtful! Isn't Her Grace thoughtful, everyone?"

Murmurs of agreement ripple through the room with varying degrees of sincerity. Josh avoids eye contact entirely, staring at his script with the intensity of a man trying to absorb its contents through osmosis.

"I've been thinking a lot about this play," I continue, moving further into the room. Joe follows, his watchful gaze sweeping across the assembled cast and crew. "About what it means, especially today. *The Taming of the Shrew* has been interpreted in so many ways over the centuries."

"Most of them misogynistic," Monica interjects with unexpected boldness, then immediately blushes at her own forwardness. "I mean... historically speaking."

"Exactly," I agree, smiling at her. "But working with wild animals for most of my life has taught me something I think applies to Katherina's story as well— there are certain creatures, certain people, who simply can't be truly tamed. They might adapt, they might compromise, they might even perform compliance when necessary. But their essential nature remains untouched, unbroken."

Brent finally turns from his reflection, his perfect eyebrows arching with interest. "Are you suggesting Katherina was never actually tamed?"

"I'm suggesting she found a way to navigate her world without surrendering her true self," I reply. "Much like many of us do in situations where we're expected to fit into roles that don't quite suit us." I make purposeful eye contact with Josh, who looks away.

Monica steps forward, her transformation into Katherina seeming to deepen before my eyes. "That's exactly how I'm playing her final speech," she says, her earlier stutter completely absent. "Many actors believe the speech is delivered with a subtle 'wink' to the audience."

"A wink?" Brent scoffs across the room.

"Yes," Monica nods eagerly. "When Katherina addresses her own mind as equal to that of others, she's not submitting — she's asserting her intelligence while appearing to comply with social expectations. She only plays at being tamed, but is never truly broken."

"I like that interpretation," I tell her, impressed by the thoughtfulness behind her approach.

"I choose to play it as if Katherina walks off stage after the play ends being even more herself— even more of a 'shrew,' if you will," Monica continues, her eyes bright with passion for her craft. "She's satisfied the immediate demand for compliance, but remains unchanged at her core."

"That's...remarkably relevant," I say, thinking of my own journey as a duchess. "Finding a way to honor both external expectations and internal truth."

A crash from the corner makes everyone jump. Cosmo has knocked over a small table while attempting to adjust a prop. As he scrambles to right it, I notice something that makes my investigative instincts flare to life: he's wearing *gloves*. Thin, almost surgical gloves that seem oddly out of place for a stage manager.

"Sorry, sorry," he mutters, gathering the fallen items. "Just finishing the final prep."

He moves to a door marked "Maintenance" and produces a key from his pocket, unlocking it with practiced ease. Inside, I glimpse rows of cleaning supplies— including several industrial bottles with hazard warnings clearly visible on their labels.

"Sorry to interrupt," Cosmo says, startled by my attention. "Just a quick wipe-down of the props and set pieces. Dust shows up terribly under the lights, you know."

"Well, I should let you all finish preparing," I say, deciding not to push further before the performance. "I just wanted to say that I believe in what you're doing here. Art matters, especially in difficult times."

"Thank you, Your Grace," Jenny gushes, clasping her hands dramatically. "Your support means everything to us."

"Break a leg, everyone," I say, using the traditional theater wish for good luck. My eyes linger for an extra moment on Josh's already broken limb, and I add, "Figuratively speaking, of course."

Josh manages a weak smile, the first I've seen from him tonight. "Thank you, Your Grace. I'll try not to break anything else."

As Joe and I turn to leave, Brent steps forward, his movement deliberately placing himself between me and the exit. "Your Grace," he says, his voice pitched to carry just to me, "I hope you enjoy the performance. I've put everything into this role."

There's something in his tone— a subtle emphasis, an underlying message I can't quite decipher. Before I can respond, Monica approaches, her fingers nervously toying with the silver "B" necklace at her throat.

"It really is an honor to perform for you," she says softly. "Especially given all that's happened."

I nod to them both, maintaining my duchess smile while mentally filing away every detail of this interaction. "The honor is mine," I reply. "I look forward to seeing your interpretation of these complex characters."

Before leaving, I move toward Josh, still sitting in his chair.

"Good luck, Josh," I say, looking straight at him.

"Thanks," he says, suddenly ashamed. I can tell, this is my moment. *It's now or never.*

"Josh," I whisper, leaning closer to him. "You were trying to tell me something before that light hit you. Please. Tell me now. So no one else gets hurt."

Josh's eyes water. He looks up at me, his cheeks pink. "Your Grace," he says, his voice shaking. "I really only said that to get you to stop the show. I'm *terrified* to perform in public. I don't know anything about who killed Tom. I just– I wanted to get out of performing."

I scan his face looking for a lie, but I don't see one there. Either Josh is telling me the truth, or he's the best actor here.

"Thank you for being honest," I say. With that, I leave Josh to his lines.

As we exit the green room, Joe's pace matches mine perfectly, his body language alert but not alarmed. I feel the weight of Officer Basilier's gun pressed into my hand as we passed in the lobby— a precaution I hope proves unnecessary, but which rests now in my clutch purse alongside my lipstick and theater program.

Tonight, the real performance isn't just on stage. It's all around us, as everyone plays their part in this elaborate dance of deception and revelation. By the final curtain call, I hope to know which of these actors has been playing the most dangerous role of all— that of a killer hiding in plain sight.

I'M BACK where I began this crazy adventure: sitting in a theatre with two hundred eyes staring at the back of my head. The velvet seats of the Monrovian Royal Theater embrace me like an old friend— albeit one who's slightly judgmental about my posture. Jack sits to my right, looking every inch the Duke in his perfectly tailored tuxedo, while Maggie and Officer Basilier flank our little royal contingent like stylishly dressed bodyguards. At our feet, Joe and Luma have arranged themselves with surprising decorum, considering they're two massive dogs in a historic theater surrounded by people in formal wear who probably don't appreciate dog hair on their evening attire. The orchestra tunes in the pit below, creating that distinctive pre-performance jumble of sounds that somehow always makes my heart race with equal parts excitement and dread.

"So," Officer Basilier leans forward, her voice low enough that only our immediate group can hear. "How did your back-stage reconnaissance go? Notice anything suspicious?"

I adjust the small clutch purse on my lap, feeling the reas-suring weight of her service weapon inside. It's both comforting and terrifying to know I'm currently armed in a theater full of Monrovia's elite.

"Josh said he was lying about knowing who killed Tom," I murmur.

"Do you believe him?"

"I do," I tell her honestly. "The rest of the cast at least pretended to listen to my speech."

Jack takes my hand, his thumb tracing small circles on my palm—a gesture that somehow grounds me amid the swirling theories and suspicions.

"The officers are in position," Officer Basilier continues. "Two backstage, four in the audience, two by each exit. If anyone makes a suspicious move, we'll be ready."

"What about the stage itself?" I ask. "After what happened to Josh..."

"I personally checked the rigging this afternoon," Officer Basilier says with quiet confidence. "No more 'accidents' from above."

"Speaking of Josh," Maggie interjects, glancing at her program. "How did he look? I'm amazed he's performing at all with his injuries."

"Terrified," I admit. "But determined, in his own way. I think he feels safer on stage than hiding somewhere alone."

"Safety in the spotlight," Jack muses. "An unusual strategy, but not without merit."

A woman behind us taps Maggie on the shoulder and offers an exaggerated "Shhh," her opera glasses glinting accusingly in the dimming house lights. I resist the childish urge to stick out my tongue and instead offer my most duchess-like apologetic nod.

The crowd around us settles into that peculiar hush of anticipation that precedes a performance. I can feel the collective expectancy building, hundreds of people preparing to be transported by the illusion about to unfold before them. None of them know they might be sitting in the same room as a murderer. The thought makes me shiver despite the theater's warmth.

"Cold?" Jack asks, misinterpreting my reaction.

"Just thinking about how strange this all is," I whisper. "Sitting here like normal theatergoers while actually waiting for a killer to reveal themselves."

Jack squeezes my hand. "You've never been a normal anything, Rebecca," he says with a smile that crinkles the corners of his eyes. "It's one of the many reasons I love you."

I turn to look at him fully, struck by the simple perfection of his statement. "Thank you for never trying to stop me from being untameable."

His smile deepens, becoming more private, meant only for me despite the hundreds of people surrounding us. "Rebecca, I love you. Why would I fall in love with you only to change you?"

The sincerity in his voice makes my chest tight with emotion. This man— this Duke— who could have had anyone, chose me, exactly as I am. No etiquette lessons or duchess training or proper protocol could ever be worth sacrificing that acceptance.

"Though," Jack adds, his voice dropping to a teasing whisper, "I WOULD really like to go on that honeymoon. Soon. Very soon. Preferably to somewhere without murderers, theatrical emergencies, or Mrs. Trechón-approved activities."

I laugh softly, leaning closer to him. "I was thinking the same thing. Actually, I wanted to tell you that I've been talking with Maggie about—"

The lights blink once, twice, then dim completely, cutting off my thought. A hush falls over the audience as the heavy velvet curtain trembles slightly, preparing to rise. The orchestra concludes their tuning with one final, unified note that hangs in the air like a promise.

Jack gives my hand one last squeeze as we settle back to watch the performance. I should be excited—this is, after all, my debut as patron of the Monrovian Royal Theater. Instead, my mind keeps returning to Cosmo in those thin gloves, unlocking the maintenance closet with practiced ease.

The curtain rises slowly, revealing a tavern scene where the drunken tinker, Christopher Sly, played by a visibly nervous Josh, lies sprawled across a bench. Despite his bandaged leg propped awkwardly before him, Josh manages to convey Sly's inebriated state convincingly. Perhaps playing drunk is easier when you're already unsteady on your feet.

As the Lord and his huntsmen discover the unconscious Sly and begin plotting their elaborate prank—convincing him he's actually a nobleman who's been mad for years—I find my attention split between the performance and my own swirling thoughts.

Industrial cleaner. Access to the maintenance closet. Gloves.

Officer Basilier's report mentioned the poison was found only in Tom's cup, not in the wine itself. Someone had to have direct access to his personal prop. Someone who could move backstage without raising suspicion.

On stage, Josh struggles through his lines, sweat visibly beading on his forehead under the harsh lights. "What, would you make me mad? Am I not Christopher Sly, old Sly's son of Burton-Heath, by birth a pedlar, by education a cardmaker, by transmutation a bear-herd, and now by present profession a tinker?"

His delivery is stilted, nervous, but something about his desperation feels authentic to the character— a man suddenly confronted with a reality that contradicts everything he believes about himself.

My mind keeps circling back to Cosmo. The man is everywhere in this theater— lighting booth, backstage, prop room. He has access to everything, knows everyone's schedule, handles all the equipment. No one would question his presence anywhere in the building.

And he's devoted to Jenny. Twenty-five years of loyal service to a director whose career has never quite reached the heights she believes she deserves. A man who would do anything to help her succeed, to give her the breakthrough she's always wanted.

A thought strikes me so suddenly I nearly gasp aloud.

Publicity.

What generates more publicity for a struggling theater production than a tragic death? Especially when that death creates a story with all the elements the press loves—a duchess patron, a murdered actor, a show that bravely "goes on" despite the tragedy.

The "Restart the Shrew" campaign. The perfectly timed website. The viral videos.

Cosmo had access to the cleaning supplies— the exact type of poison found in Tom's cup. He had opportunity, access to all areas of the theater without suspicion. And he had motive: helping Jenny achieve the recognition she's always craved.

But there's one more piece that suddenly clicks into place. Jenny mentioned that Tom's role was small but pivotal — the kind of role that wouldn't be missed by casual theatergoers if replaced by an understudy, but important enough that his death would generate sympathy and interest.

The perfect victim for a publicity stunt gone horribly wrong.

And then Josh— who knew something, who was about to tell us everything—conveniently silenced by a falling light. A light that would have been rigged by the same person who manages all the technical aspects of the production.

On stage, the players are now performing the play-within-a-play for the bewildered Christopher Sly. The introduction of Petruchio and Katherina is minutes away. Monica will soon make her entrance as the titular shrew, transformed from her timid self into the fierce, untameable character she so brilliantly embodies.

But I can't wait. Every second we sit here is another second that a killer stands in the wings, perhaps planning their next move. What if Josh isn't the only one who knows too much? What if someone else is in danger?

I lean over to whisper my revelation to Officer Basilier, but she's already focused intently on the backstage area, her hand hovering near her evening purse where I know her backup weapon rests.

"I need to stop this now," I whisper to Jack.

His eyes widen in alarm. "Rebecca, what—"

But I'm already moving, sliding past his knees, ignoring the indignant huffs of the people I disturb. Joe immediately rises to follow me, sensing my urgency even without a command.

"Rebecca!" Maggie hisses, but I'm beyond caring about protocol or propriety.

The stage is only feet away from our front-row seats. Before anyone can stop me, I hoist myself up onto the polished wooden boards, my formal gown hampering the movement just enough to make it less graceful than I'd hoped.

The audience gasps collectively, a sound like a sudden gust of wind through autumn leaves. The actors freeze mid-scene, their expressions a comical mixture of shock and confusion.

Josh, still sprawled on his makeshift throne as the bewildered Christopher Sly, actually lets out an audible sigh of relief. "Thank God," he whispers, just loud enough for me to hear.

I turn to face the audience, hundreds of bewildered faces staring back at me like I've just sprouted a second head. In the front row, Jack looks both horrified and oddly proud, while Officer Basilier is already on her feet, hand inside her purse.

Maggie has covered her eyes with one hand, though I can see her peeking through her fingers.

"Ladies and gentlemen," I announce, finding my new duchess-voice— the one that carries authority even when I feel anything but authoritative. "I apologize for this interruption, but I must ask you to stop the play."

The murmurs ripple through the crowd, growing in volume. I raise my hand, and to my surprise, the theater falls silent again.

"I know who killed Tom Prink," I declare, my voice ringing through the hushed theater. "And I believe they may be planning to strike again tonight."

From the wings, I hear a commotion—the sound of something metallic clattering to the floor, followed by rapid footsteps. Officer Basilier is already moving, signaling to her undercover officers positioned throughout the theater.

Josh struggles to his feet beside me, wincing as he puts weight on his injured leg. "It's Cosmo," he says, his voice carrying in the stunned silence. "Cosmo cut the rope that dropped the light on me. I saw him do it, but I was too afraid to say anything. He said he'd hurt Brent if I told anyone."

The audience erupts in confused chatter, some thinking this is part of the show, others realizing with dawning horror that they're witnessing something all too real.

"Please remain calm and stay in your seats," I address the crowd, trying to project a confidence I don't entirely feel. "The police are here, and they have the situation under control."

As if to contradict me, a crash sounds from backstage, followed by a woman's scream— Jenny's voice, I realize with a jolt. Joe barks once, sharply, then bounds up onto the stage beside me, his massive form somehow making the entire situation seem both more chaotic and more secure.

"Rebecca!" Jack calls, now standing at the edge of the stage. "Be careful!"

CHAPTER
Nineteen

I STAND CENTER STAGE, feeling hundreds of eyes boring into me like I'm a zoo animal that's suddenly learned to tap dance. The theater's silence holds a weight to it— the collective breath-holding of Monrovia's elite as they try to process the sight of their newest Duchess interrupting Shakespeare. Joe plants himself firmly beside me, his massive form somehow lending legitimacy to my theatrical hijacking. I've spent my career interpreting animal behavior, but right now, I'm banking on my ability to read humans who are far more dangerous than any predator I've trained.

"Ladies and gentlemen," I continue, finding strength in the absurdity of the situation. "I apologize for the interruption, but as your duchess and the patron of this theater, I cannot in good conscience allow this performance to continue without addressing what happened to Tom Prink."

A murmur ripples through the audience like wind across tall grass. In the front row, Jack's expression hovers somewhere between horror and pride— the look of a man who knew exactly what he was getting into when he married me but is still occasionally surprised by the specifics.

"As many of you know, Tom Prink was murdered.

Poisoned with industrial cleaner that was added to his prop on stage." I let this sink in, watching faces shift from confusion to shock. "What you may not know is that someone also attempted to silence Josh Thoroughgood by dropping a stage light on him when he was about to reveal what he knew."

I gesture to Josh, who stands awkwardly beside me, his bandaged leg a visible reminder of how close he came to joining Tom.

"Over the past week, I've been working as a Royal Investigator. My partner Maggie and I had Officer Basilier's blessing to work with the Police to uncover who would want to kill a beloved actor in a small theatrical production." I sweep my hand toward the audience where Officer Basilier rises slightly from her seat, her eyes never leaving the wings where I know she's tracking movement. "And I believe I know who did it, and why."

The audience leans forward collectively, like a single organism suddenly riveted. I'd laugh at how theatrical this all is if someone's life wasn't at stake.

"At first, I suspected Brent Thoroughgood."

A gasp rises from several sections of the audience. I press on before the whispers can build.

"The reasoning was simple— publicity. What better way to draw attention to a production than a tragedy involving its star? The press coverage alone has been worth thousands in free advertising. The 'Restart the Shrew' campaign went viral. Ticket sales skyrocketed." I pause, letting the logic of this sink in. "Brent stood to gain the most from this production's success. It was meant to be his triumphant return to the stage after years in film."

The curtain behind me rustles, and Brent Thoroughgood steps out, his movie-star features arranged in an expression of dignified indignation. His entrance is so perfectly timed it's hard not to applaud his theatrical instinct— even now, he understands dramatic timing.

"I feel I must address these allegations directly," he announces, his rich voice projecting effortlessly without seeming to try. The mark of years of training. "While I appreciate Her Grace's diligence in seeking justice for Tom, I can assure you I had no hand in his death."

He turns to face the audience fully, a slight tremor in his hand the only crack in his perfect facade.

"However, since Her Grace has made my private matters a subject of public speculation, I might as well set the record straight." He draws a deep breath. "I am indeed facing the end of my acting career, though not by choice. I have a degenerative condition affecting my mobility. Within two years, I will likely require assistance to walk. Within five, I may be confined to a wheelchair."

The audience's collective intake of breath is audible. I hadn't expected Brent to make such a public admission, and for a moment, I feel a stab of guilt for forcing his hand.

"This production was to be my farewell to the stage— a chance to perform while I still can, to remind the world that I am more than just an action star." His voice catches slightly, a vulnerability I hadn't thought him capable of displaying. "I needed this play to succeed, yes. But I would never have sacrificed Tom's life for publicity. He was a friend."

Brent turns to look at me, his expression a masterclass in wounded dignity. "Is that explanation sufficient, Your Grace? Or shall I bare more of my personal tragedy for the court of public opinion?"

The sarcasm is subtle but unmistakable. I incline my head slightly, acknowledging both his point and his pain.

"Thank you for your honesty, Mr. Thoroughgood," I say, genuinely moved despite my lingering suspicions. "And I apologize for forcing such a personal disclosure."

I turn back to the audience. "I thought, perhaps, Monica, who plays the role of Katherina and the Hostess, might have killed Tom to support Brent—"

Monica gasps from behind the onstage bar, her hand flying to the necklace with the letter B around her throat.

"You are in love with him, aren't you Monica?"

"Love is a big word," Monica flushes. "But– you could say that we're very close–"

"We're dating," Brent shouts across the stage. "I love her. I gave her the necklace."

"But I would never kill anyone!" Monica urgently clarifies.

"I agree," I tell her. "Monica isn't capable of killing anyone. My suspicions next fell to Josh Thoroughgood."

Josh flinches beside me, his Adam's apple bobbing nervously as he swallows.

"The logic was simple but inverted— I thought perhaps Josh wanted to sabotage the production to protect his brother from worsening his condition through the rigors of performance." I glance at Josh, whose eyes widen with surprise at this theory. "Or perhaps he felt pressured into a role he wasn't ready for, one that would expose him to public ridicule when he inevitably failed to match his brother's talent."

"I—I would never," Josh stammers, his voice cracking. "I mean, yes, I didn't want this role. I'm terrible, as everyone can plainly see. But I wouldn't kill someone! I was terrified someone was going to get hurt, that's why I wanted the production shut down!"

"I believe you, Josh," I say gently. "Which is why my investigation continued."

I take a step closer to the edge of the stage, narrowing the gap between myself and the audience. "My attention then turned to Jenny Jay, our ambitious director."

From her seat in the third row, Jenny rises halfway, her face flushed with indignation.

"This is outrageous!" she protests. "I have devoted my life to the theater! To suggest I would harm anyone for—"

"For publicity?" I interject smoothly. "For the chance to finally break through after decades of toiling in regional theater? For a production that would cement your reputation as a director who can overcome tragedy and still deliver art?"

Jenny's mouth opens and closes several times, like a fish suddenly finding itself on land. "I... that's not... how dare you!"

"I dare because two people have been hurt," I reply, my voice hardening. "One of them fatally. And the person responsible is still in this theater."

The tension in the room ratchets up another notch. I can feel Joe shifting beside me, his massive head swiveling as he monitors the reactions around us.

"Jenny," I continue, softening my tone slightly, "I don't believe you killed Tom. But I do believe the killer acted, in part, because of their feelings for you."

Her confusion appears genuine. "What on earth are you talking about?"

"I'm talking about the person who has been by your side for twenty-five years. The person who takes on any job you need, no matter how menial or demanding. The person who looks at you the way my Joe looks at a perfectly grilled steak." I pause, letting my gaze drift upward to the lighting booth. "I'm talking about Cosmo Flap."

The spotlight operator flinches, illuminated in his own booth like an actor caught in his light.

"Cosmo has access to every area of this theater," I continue, projecting my voice to reach the back row. "He holds the keys to all the maintenance closets, including the one containing industrial cleaning supplies— the exact type used to poison Tom. He manages the rigging for the lights— the same rigging that 'mysteriously' failed and nearly killed Josh when he was trying to convince me not to allow the play to continue. Because the play not continuing would devastate Jenny. And *Jenny* is all Cosmo cares about."

Cosmo's face, visible from the booth, has gone ashen. Even from this distance, I can see the panic setting in.

"But what truly convinced me was the motive," I say, looking directly at Jenny now. "Cosmo has been in love with you for decades, Jenny. Everything he does is to support your dreams, your ambitions. When this production was struggling to gain attention, what better way to help than to create a tragic story that would generate endless publicity? The mourning director bravely continuing despite tragedy. The viral campaign. The sold-out performances."

The theater has gone utterly silent. Even breathing seems too loud in this moment.

"Tom's role was perfect for this plan— small enough that an understudy could take over without significantly impacting the production, but important enough that his death would generate sympathy and interest." I turn back toward the lighting booth. "Isn't that right, Cosmo?"

From the stage, Jenny calls out toward the lighting booth. "Cosmo? Tell me it isn't true!"

There's a sudden commotion in the booth— the sound of equipment being knocked over, a door slamming. Officer Basilier is already moving, signaling to her officers stationed throughout the theater. "I love you, Jenny! I've always loved you! I'll find you again!" Cosmo's shout comes from the back of the theatre.

"He's running!" someone calls from the wings.

Joe barks once, sharply, then bounds from the stage with astonishing grace for a dog his size. He disappears into the wings, following some scent or sound I can't detect.

"Please remain calm," I tell the audience, trying to project a confidence I don't entirely feel. "The police have the building surrounded."

From backstage comes a series of crashes, followed by shouting and the unmistakable sound of Joe's deep, authoritative bark. A moment later, Officer Basilier's voice rings out: "POLICE! STOP RIGHT THERE!"

The audience is no longer seated— people stand, craning

their necks, some moving toward the exits while others push closer to the stage, hungry for drama that's not part of the scheduled performance.

I hold my ground at center stage, heart pounding. Josh looks like he might faint beside me, while Brent stands unnaturally still, his actor's training allowing him to remain composed even in chaos.

Suddenly, the backstage door bursts open, and Officer Basilier emerges, firmly gripping Cosmo's arms behind his back. His mustache droops pathetically, his eyes wild with panic. Two uniformed officers flank them, and Joe prances behind, looking immensely pleased with himself.

"We got him," Officer Basilier announces, her voice carrying through the theater without effort. "And he had these." She holds up a pair of thin surgical gloves. "Along with this." In her other hand is a bottle of cleaner, a hazard sign on the front.

Cosmo's shoulders slump in defeat. "It wasn't supposed to be like this," he says, his voice barely audible. "Tom was supposed to be the only one. Just enough to get attention for the show." His gaze finds Jenny, who stands frozen in horror near her seat. "I just wanted you to finally get the recognition you deserved. Twenty-five years, Jenny. Twenty-five years watching you pour your heart into productions that no one cared about. Can't you see? This was the only way to get people to pay attention to your work."

Jenny's hands cover her mouth, her eyes wide with horror. "Cosmo," she whispers. "What have you done?"

"Everything," he says simply. "I've done everything for you. The props, the lights, the costumes, the sets." His voice breaks. "Everything to make your vision come true. I never expected the Duchess would cancel the play!"

"Alright lover boy," Officer Basilier says grimly, tightening her grip on his arm. "Let's go."

"It was for you, Jenny!" Cosmo shouts as he's drug out of the theatre. "It was all for you!"

As the officers lead Cosmo away, a stunned silence falls over the theater. Then, inevitably, the press in attendance begin shouting questions, cameras flash, and the orderly audience dissolves into a churning mass of speculation and excitement.

I take a deep breath, suddenly aware of how exhausted I feel. Josh gives me a shaky smile of gratitude before limping off stage, likely in search of somewhere quiet to process everything that's happened.

Looking out at the chaos, I decide to give the press what they want— one final statement before I escape.

"You can call me the Duchess of Death if you want," I announce, raising my voice above the din. "But at least I'm being royal MY way."

With that, I hop down from the stage, landing with less grace than I'd like in these heels. Jack is waiting, his arms open to catch me.

"That," he says as I fall against his chest, "was both the most terrifying and impressive thing I've ever seen."

I laugh, the sound muffled against his shirt. "Sorry to hijack Shakespeare."

"I think he'd approve. Much more exciting than the original ending." Jack pulls back just enough to look into my eyes. "Though I'd prefer if my wife didn't make a habit of confronting murderers from center stage."

"Actually," I say, a smile spreading across my face, "you'll be glad to know I've planned our escape from the oncoming publicity storm." I tap his chest lightly. "Pack your bags, Duke. We're finally taking that honeymoon." I reach into my clutch and pull out two train tickets.

Jack's face lights up with genuine delight. "Really? Where are we going?"

"That," I say, pressing a kiss to his lips, "is a surprise. But I promise it involves a vacation, absolutely zero murders, and not a single etiquette lesson."

"Sounds perfect," he sighs, drawing me closer. "Just us, some peace and quiet—"

"And no investigations," I finish for him.

Joe and Luma choose this moment to express their approval, barking joyfully as they circle around us. Their enthusiasm draws smiles even from the nearby officers securing the scene.

"Do you really think we can go somewhere without a murder following us?" Jack asks, only half-joking.

Maggie, appearing beside us with perfect timing, snorts softly. "Unlikely," she mutters, but her smile takes the sting from her words.

I laugh, leaning into Jack's embrace as reporters continue shouting questions from every direction. Let them call me the Duchess of Death. Let Mrs. Trechón despair over my unconventional approach to royalty. For now, I've caught a killer, saved a life or two, and secured a honeymoon with the man I love.

And one thing's for sure: whether I'm a duchess, or a Royal Investigator, or an animal trainer, I'm a woman who will never– *ever*– be tamed.

———

For an excerpt from Book 8 in the Rebecca Orange Castle Cozy Mystery Series, "A Christmas Crime," keep reading!

A Christmas Crime

Trains are peaceful, I think to myself. *I could get used to this.* Beneath my feet, the click-clack of wheels over metal vibrates through my legs. Over the past twenty-four hours, the sound has become a soothing one. I didn't expect to like traveling by train so much, but there's something nostalgic and quaint about it. It's the perfect mode of transportation for my Christmas-time honeymoon with Jack.

The honeymoon suite of the *Monrovian Royal Express* lurches gently as our train climbs higher into the mountains, snow-covered pines rushing past panoramic windows. Beside me, Joe— my 250-pound Tibetan Mastiff dog— leans into my leg, letting out an enormous burp. Next to him, an empty silver bowl that contained caviar just moments ago rattles in pace.

"Joe, there's no burping in the honeymoon suite," I say, taking a sip of champagne from the flute in my hand. Next to Joe, Luma— the Duke's collie, who's just finished her own bowl of caviar— picks up a paw and boops Joe on the nose, as if she's enforcing Royal behavior. She gives him a look that says, *can you try to act dignified for once?*

Joe burps again in response.

Beside me, the Duke— Jack— my *husband,* which still feels strange to say— raises his glass to mine. He clinks the glasses together, wearing that quiet smile that made me fall for him in the first place.

"Actually," Jack corrects me, "I think the Duke and Duchess of Atwood passed a law saying dog burps are *encouraged* on trains. Didn't you hear? They just got married this year, if you believe the tabloids." He winks at me, telling our own story as if it belongs to strangers.

The Duke and Duchess, I think. Royal titles are another concept I'm still getting used to, like having security follow you everywhere and using multiple forks at dinner.

"I heard the Duke is quite handsome," I say, taking another sip of my champagne. "But I don't follow tabloids much."

"Your first lie to me. A good sign for our marriage, I think," Jack says, his eyes crinkling at the corners. He knows I love a good tabloid, preferably read in a bubble bath and full of questionable gossip.

Joe lets out a grumble of contentment as he licks the last bits of caviar from his tiny silver dish. Then, he moves his massive golden bulk to sprawl across a velvet ottoman that's probably an antique from some royal collection. Next to him, Luma curls up more daintily on her own cushion. Her eyes dart between all of us as if she's waiting for a Royal attendant to brush her fur.

"She's going to get spoiled," I say, nodding toward Luma. "She fits the Royal lifestyle more than any of us do."

Jack laughs. "Says the woman who has Chef Renauld prepare her dog a Prince's meal every night."

I reach over to scratch Joe behind his ears, and he lets out a contented sigh. "Joe's earned it. Getting in trouble all the time is hard work."

The honeymoon suite is over-decorated in the best

possible way. Wood-paneled walls inlaid with gold. Plush burgundy seating. A dining nook, a separate bedroom visible through French doors, and even a small bathroom with— I kid you not— a clawfoot tub. The windows stretch from floor to ceiling, offering unobstructed views of the mountain land-scape. It's like someone took a five-star hotel room and shrunk it down to fit on a train.

"This is nice," I say, leaning into Jack's shoulder. "Just us. No staff, no royal duties. We finally get some time alone—"

Just then, the door to our compartment slides open, and a familiar voice fills the cabin.

"Can you believe how big the waffles are?" Maggie exclaims, standing in the doorway with wide eyes. "We just got room service and they're as big as my head!"

Jack laughs, his arm tightening around my shoulders. "Well... *almost* alone."

I shoot him a look that's half amusement, half exaspera-tion. When we planned this honeymoon, I had visions of just the two of us cuddled up in front of a fireplace, sipping hot chocolate, and generally doing the things newlyweds do. I should have known better. Being a Royal means you can never be truly alone.

Maggie steps fully into our compartment, her blonde braids bouncing with each movement. She's traded her usual professional attire for a casual sweater and jeans, but still manages to look like she could organize a gala at a moment's notice. Her tablet is tucked under her arm— the electronic appendage she's never without.

"Sorry to interrupt," she says, not looking sorry at all. "But I wanted to check if you'd like breakfast delivered here or if you're planning to join us in the dining car?" Her eyes drift to the champagne and caviar. "Although I see you've already started."

"It's our honeymoon, Maggie," I say pointedly.

"I know, I know! And I promise Benjamin and I will stay

completely out of your way." She mimes zipping her lips, then immediately unzips them to continue. "Besides, the Queen said it was either me or members of the Royal Guard, so I'm the better choice, right?"

Jack sighs with good humor. "She's not wrong."

I can't argue with that. When Jack had shared that we were planning a honeymoon without security, his aunt (the Queen) practically had a coronary. As third in line for the Monrovian throne, Jack rarely goes anywhere without protection. After some loud whispering, they ultimately agreed on a compromise: Maggie would escort us on the trip as Royal liaison, reporting back and managing any security issues. The compromise felt like a win: I trust Maggie to be less obtrusive than Royal Guards, and it doesn't hurt having my best friend on the trip.

"Although," Maggie adds, shifting her weight from one foot to the other in that way she does when she's about to drop news she knows I won't like, "the Queen *did* insist I bring a little muscle along. She said she didn't feel confident I'd be able to handle terrorist threats and potential kidnappers on my own..."

"But you're so tough!" I add solemnly.

"Apparently not tough enough. So I had to ask for some help..."

She gestures toward the hallway behind her. A familiar voice floats in before we see its owner.

"These croissants are extraordinary. The butter actually tastes like butter, not that garbage they serve at the station."

Officer Basilier steps into view, and I nearly choke on my champagne. She's wearing flannel pajamas printed with tiny handcuffs and police badges, her short hair sticking up at odd angles. She's holding a croissant in one hand and a steaming mug in the other.

"Officer Basilier?" I splutter. "What are you doing here?" When we boarded the train last night, I thought Maggie and her new boyfriend— Benjamin, who owns the pet store in the village— were our only company.

Joe perks up at the sight of Officer Basilier, his tail thumping against the ottoman. For reasons I've never fully understood, my massive dog adores the petite police officer.

"Royal security," she says, taking a bite of her croissant and speaking through it. "Queen's orders. The Duke needs protection, even on his honeymoon." She gestures vaguely with her croissant. "Third in line for the throne and all that. And then you have to go and marry him and make everything even more public and weird. Might as well have painted a target on both your backs, Orange."

Jack leans forward, setting his champagne flute on the table, his expression surly. "I wasn't informed of this! Maggie, I must insist—"

"It's too late, the next station is our stop!" Maggie says, throwing her hands in the air before muttering, "This is why I waited to tell you until the train was too far gone..."

"Don't worry," Officer Basilier replies, brushing croissant crumbs from her pajama top. "I'll stay out of your way. It's *her* you need to worry about." She jerks her thumb toward Maggie, who looks affronted.

"Me? I'm the definition of discretion!"

Jack and I exchange a look that sends us both into laughter. Maggie's many talents don't include being discreet.

"I'll be in the breakfast car if anyone needs me," Officer Basilier announces, turning to leave. "Though I sincerely hope no one does. I need a vacation every now and then, too, you know..."

As she disappears down the corridor, I turn to Maggie with raised eyebrows. "Anyone else hiding in the train that I should know about? The royal gardener? The Queen's third cousin twice removed?"

"Just Benjamin," she says brightly, smiling at the mention of her love interest, who runs the pet store in Atwood Village.

"He's finishing his waffle and boring me with facts about what movies were shot in the small town we're heading to."

Luma trots over to the door, peering out as if hoping to catch a glimpse of more visitors, then returns to curl up next to Joe on the ottoman. The dogs, at least, seem unfazed by our growing entourage.

Maggie makes herself comfortable on one of the plush armchairs, pulling out her tablet. "Speaking of, I've been doing more research on where we're going, and it's absolutely magical."

I can't help but feel a flicker of excitement at Maggie's research. I'd picked the Château des Flocons after stumbling across it online— a fairytale castle perched on a snowy mountain, converted into a boutique ski resort. I knew immediately it was the perfect spot for a honeymoon.

"It's an old castle that's been in the same family for generations," Maggie continues, swiping through images on her tablet. "The current owner, Mr. Jacoby, inherited the title of Lord but prefers to be called Mister. He's like you, Jack," Maggie nods. "He likes to think of himself as a regular person."

"That's me," Jack laughs, throwing his hands in the air. "Just constantly thinking of myself as an ordinary person!"

"The castle has seven bedrooms total," Maggie continues. "One for Mr. Jacoby, one for his manager Freya, one for *her* son, and four for guests. You'll have the best suite, of course," Maggie adds, as if there was any question.

"It looks smaller than Castle Atwood," I observe, glancing at the photos over Maggie's shoulder.

"Much smaller," she agrees. "More intimate. And completely charming. The manager— Freya— has done all the interior decorating— lots of bookshelves, plush furniture, warm lighting. It's cozy rather than grand."

That sounds perfect to me. After months of living in the sprawling Castle Atwood with its countless rooms and corridors, something more human-sized appeals to my American sensibilities.

"And it's walking distance to Floconville Village," Maggie continues. "The most adorable little mountain town you've ever seen. Cobblestone streets, cafes, pubs, the works. Everything's decorated for Christmas right now."

Jack slides closer to me on the sofa. "It sounds perfect." His hand finds mine, our fingers intertwining naturally.

"Oh!" Maggie's eyes widen with excitement. "And the best part— Mr. Jacoby has given us tickets to the Glacial Games!"

"The what now?" I ask.

"The Glacial Games! Only the biggest winter sports competition in Monrovia!" Maggie looks at me like I've just admitted to never having heard of Christmas. "It's happening right on the slopes behind the château. Skiers from all over Europe compete. Benjamin is beside himself with excitement."

Of course he is. Benjamin is obsessed with all things athletic and adventurous— a byproduct of his fixation on American movies.

"Convenient, isn't it?" I ask, arching an eyebrow. "*You* wanted to see the Glacial Games and just happen to go on our honeymoon with us?"

Maggie has the grace to look slightly embarrassed. "The Queen really *did* insist I come along," she protests. "The tickets are just a... happy coincidence!"

"Mhm," I hum, unconvinced.

"Don't worry," she hastens to add. "Benjamin and I will be at the games most of the time. You won't even know we're there."

"Except at breakfast," Jack points out. "And apparently when room service delivers oversized waffles."

"Well, yes, except then." Maggie stands, clutching her tablet to her chest. "I knew you wouldn't want tickets, Rebecca, because you hate sports, but if you two decide you do want to come I can ask Mr. Jacoby to request—"

"No thanks," I tell her, shaking my head. "We just want a honeymoon with privacy. And no murder."

"Cheers to that!" Jack says.

Maggie nods, packing up her tablet. "Anyway, I should get back to Benjamin before he orders more food. The train staff are starting to give him looks."

As she heads toward the door, she pauses. "Oh, did I mention the château has issues with the plumbing? Mr. Jacoby said something always seems to be breaking due to the building's age. But the location makes up for it! It will still be a super romantic honeymoon even if there's sewage involved. Don't worry."

With that parting informational bomb, she's gone, sliding the compartment door closed behind her.

I turn to Jack, who's watching me with amusement dancing in his eyes. "So much for our private getaway," I say.

He pulls me closer, pressing a kiss to my temple. "We'll find our moments. Look at it this way," he gestures toward the window, where the snow-covered landscape continues to pass by. "We're headed to a beautiful château in the mountains. There will be skiing, hot chocolate by the fire, Christmas decorations everywhere..."

"Faulty plumbing and possible sewage," I add.

"That too." He laughs. "But we'll be together. That's what matters."

Joe lifts his massive head from the ottoman, letting out a soft woof of agreement. Luma, not to be outdone, gives a delicate bark of her own.

"See? Even the dogs agree." Jack refills our champagne flutes. "To our unconventional honeymoon. May it be memorable for all the right reasons."

I clink my glass against his, letting myself relax into the moment. "To our unconventional honeymoon."

As we sip our champagne, I gaze out at the winter wonderland passing by outside. The train climbs higher, carrying us toward the Château des Flocons, our eccentric entourage, and whatever adventures await us in the snowy mountains of Monrovia.

———

To keep reading, look for "A Christmas Crime," available in paperback!

More From Valerie Brandy

AVAILABLE NOW IN PAPERBACK:

The Rebecca Orange Castle Cozy Mystery Series:

1. Mystery at Monrovia Castle
2. A Victim in the Village
3. A Royal Ruse
4. A Kidnapped Collie
5. A Perilous Proposal
6. Murder at the Masquerade
7. A Poisonous Play
8. A Christmas Crime

The Private Investigator Annie Hudson Mystery Series:

1. Murder Behind the Gates
2. Murder in the Penthouse
3. Murder on the Farm
4. Murder in the Commune
5. Murder in the Desert
6. Murder in the Hometown

The Predator / Prey Thriller Series:

1. Trail of Obsession
2. Lies Run Deep
3. The Trap is Set
4. Woman in the Wind

Letter From the Author

Dear Reader,

Thank you for dedicating your time to the world of Monrovia and Rebecca Orange! These books mean so much to me, and my hope is always that what I've written gives you the chance to escape to a cozy new place.

I love hearing from readers (seriously, it makes the job so fun!). Please reach out to me anytime by visiting www.valeriebrandy.com or finding me on social media, even if it's just to say "hi" or talk about flower names for coffee. Monrovia is special because of the community there, and I love forming the same cozy friendships around my books.

You can also join my author club mailing list for free give-aways and updates on new releases. Scan the QR Code below or visit my website to join!

Warmly,

— Valerie Brandy